# STAYING WITH IT

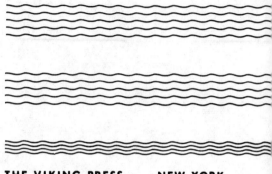

THE VIKING PRESS   NEW YORK

# STAYING WITH IT

# JOHN JEROME

Portions of this book appeared originally in *American Health,
Car and Driver, Harvard Magazine, Outside, Running, Sportstyle,*
and *United Magazine* in different form.

LIBRARY OF CONGRESS CATALOGING IN PUBLICATION DATA
Jerome, John.
    Staying with it.
    1. Athletics.   2. Swimming.   3 Middle age.
4. Physical education and training.   I. Title.
GV706.8.J47   1984      613.7'1      83-40226
ISBN 0-670-66876-1

Grateful acknowledgment is made to the following for
permission to reprint copyrighted material:
    *Croom Helm Ltd. Publishers:* Selections from Chapter Five of
*Physical Activity and Aging* by Roy J. Shepherd.
    *Plenum Publishing Corp.:* Selections from *Guide to Fitness
After Fifty* by Raymond Harris and Lawrence Frankel.

Printed in the United States of America
Set in Garamond
Designed by Ann Gold

For Amanda Vaill, who saw it whole;
for Chris, who endured it; and for
Chris's brother, who won't get it.

*"How much happiness is gained, and how much misery escaped, by frequent and violent agitation of the body."*
—Dr. Samuel Johnson

# CONTENTS

## BOOK THREE: THE PAY

# BOOK ONE
## THE JOB

# THROWING

T H E   F A M I L Y   D O G loves to chase the wormy apples that litter the ground in the fall. I toss them low, with a looping underhand throw that sends them skipping down the road to give the dog maximum action. Now and then I have the urge to reach back and fire off a true, hard throw, but I squelch the impulse. When I do try to throw properly, overhand, I'm shocked at my own stiffness. My fifty-year-old arm is like wood, my torso awkward as a cardboard box. I throw as if I'm standing in a small room.

When I was a kid I would see old folks move that way and think *they've forgotten how.* They're so old they can't remember how to throw anymore. Now I smile at that childhood misapprehension. I remember perfectly well how to throw, how I used to throw. I used to throw as mindlessly as a dog trots, easy as rain. I threw all the time, whenever I was outdoors. As kids, we threw rocks at fence posts, telephone poles, mailboxes, signposts, anything. We didn't throw to mar, to vandalize, although that was often the result. We threw to see if we could hit what we aimed at. The world offered target practice, and we just used it, as kids will.

We would line old whiskey bottles on the mud bank under the bridge, retreat to the far side, and, in our own private shooting gallery, spend afternoons firing away. Better yet was to set a tin-can target on a plank and launch it downriver, letting it drift to the limits of our range. Then we would loft long, high trajectories—fantasy artillery fire at passing enemy gunboats—at the limits of our twelve-year-old throwing arms. The rare hit would make us chuckle with pleasure, and launch another plank. ·

There was always a baseball and a couple of mitts around the house, and on summer evenings my father and I would play catch. It was the only sport I ever saw him attempt. We'd flip the ball back and forth, starting close to each other, backing slowly as he warmed up, gradually increasing the force on the throw. He'd stop to take off his shirt, ceremoniously hanging it on a backyard shrub, and then continue, his scrawny arms sticking out from his thin-strapped, 1930s undershirt. After awhile he'd start to bear down a bit, the throws coming harder, the ball starting to sizzle and pop. He had a good arm and relished using it. It wasn't practice for baseball, not preparation for athletics, it was just playing catch. It may not have happened a dozen times in my lifetime, but I remember it as every evening, all summer long. The feel of it in my shoulder and forearm still comes back to me.

It's eerie the way those sensations linger. I remember what it was like to get hot and loose, my arm ready to throw forever, quick as rubber. Trying to throw harder, I would reach so far that my arm whipped in a small circle behind my back at the beginning of the throw. And then I would drive hard off my back leg, whipping my spine forward so that my body got ahead of my arm, so that all my weight was committed to the throw before my arm followed. Segment by segment I can feel the throw uncoil—shoulder, upper arm, forearm, wrist, hand, and a final, culminating fillip of force from the fingers themselves. I loved to throw. I remember sinking into a black funk over college studies, driving out to the river, and throwing rocks for an hour, working off steam before returning to my books.

That was about the time I first noticed that throwing could hurt my arm. As I gained full height and weight I discovered that if I didn't throw regularly, I got sore. I had to start learning a gradual approach, an attitude toward my body that I'd never needed before. Childhood always permitted all-out, carefree effort. That was changing, and it puzzled me. What was going on? Had I grown too big?

It was just age. The strength to accomplish things was becoming the strength to hurt myself. On TV some vandal throws a tennis ball into the outfield at the ball game. The expensive ballplayer picks it up and attempts to throw it off the playing surface. "He'd better watch out," says the ex-ballplayer announcer. "He'll throw his arm away." I remember that. Your arm is set for a certain resistance. Switch to too light a missile and everything fires off too quickly, too hard, hurting. You have to squeeze off a throw the way you squeeze off a rifle shot, getting the motion underway, aligned, before you put real muscle behind it. The weight you throw is what you push against, the resistance that makes the motion controllable. Reduce the resistance too abruptly and things will fly apart.

That's what scares me, I think. The movements are still somewhere in my arm and torso; it's the network that holds it all together that I don't trust anymore. The containment. These days if I sit still too long, my joints take a set like hair that has been slept on wrong. I'm always fidgeting against that stiffness, working away against the little twinges that scurry from joint to joint but never quite leave. Something no longer holds me together right.

Stiffness isn't the reason why I can't throw anymore, fear

is. I picture the anatomy of my arm too well. There are things in there that don't want anything to do with quickness. Everything that makes the motion is still there, but the starting and stopping of the motion require efforts that have become scary.

Puttering around on the back porch, I come across an old bathing cap, cracked and gummy from oxidation. The surface is crazed from disuse, but underneath there is rubber that still wants to stretch, to rebound. It doesn't look as if it's much good anymore, but I don't throw it out.

# T W O
# DOWNSLOPE

IT IS A SPRING morning in the mid-1970s, and I have just come in from a slow run through the countryside near my house in New England. I am padding about the kitchen in shorts and bare feet, cooling down. I am not a daily runner— I tend to quit and start over again, just like most other guilt-ridden middle-aged exercisers—but this time circumstances have kept me going out regularly for a few weeks, and I'm beginning to reap some benefits.

I am not in the habit of noticing the physiological transactions underway in my body, but I can feel that my heart rate, recently elevated by the run, has now begun to drop appreciably. My body core is still slightly overheated, my skin flushed, my blood circulation radiating metabolic heat from the skin surface. A light sweat leaves my skin feeling salty; I'm looking forward to a hot shower. My joints and muscles are still lubricated, easy. I feel relaxed, loose, available for movement. This isn't my habitual state.

As I sit with a cup of coffee, I sense an underlying aerobic buzz, a kind of physiological hum that has been there for some time but that I never quite allowed myself to notice. I feel very good. It's a thought that stops me in my tracks, that makes me look down at myself as if checking out my arms and legs. I don't really recall feeling *good* before—not quite in this way, not in a positive flush of physical pleasure. Could I have reached my late forties without ever feeling good before? Perhaps some neurotic quirk prevented this pleasure from getting to my attention? Or maybe the pleasure is really the product of physical effort, which in the past I have avoided when possible. Maybe until now, feeling good was too much trouble.

I only ran for a couple of years, but I still catch myself being defensive about it. Runners catch a lot of grief. It stems from the fairly common judgment that sports aren't serious enough, or one's physical state important enough, to warrant all that time and attention. (Newspaper staffs usually refer to the sports desk as the toy department.) I guess my defensiveness is in reaction to that attitude.

I had to run, however. For an earlier book I spent some years studying the physiology of athletics, and I found that time to be powerfully entertaining as well as illuminating. I wanted to continue the entertainment. But also, the literature of physiology kept promising me magic, and I wanted some of that magic to happen to me. I began running distrustingly, and hated it for a long time, keeping at it only out of an ingenuous faith in science and the printed word. Then I began to like it. I'm lucky enough to live in the country and work at home. I could slip away any time I wanted for a fresh-air break, down a back road with no traffic and no barking dogs. That was fine.

Nowhere in the running literature do they quite prepare you for the startling suddenness of the training effect. You may be unable to run a quarter of a mile when you begin, but push yourself only a little and within days you double or triple the distance. In the beginning, the increase from the training effect can be measured literally in yards, day by day. It happens so quickly, with so little real discomfort, that most of us find it more than thrilling. It is a prediction of a personal future that is in direct contradiction to almost every other signal that our bodies give. Those signals—the little aches and pains and, mostly, simple fatigue—seem to be warnings that we should stop doing whatever we're doing. Training tells us we may continue.

As a runner I got that far and then some, far enough to foresee a string of intriguing possibilities. I learned that I had barely begun to understand physiology, and that the physiology texts only hinted at what might be done. At the same time running, because it loads and pounds the joints so constantly, turned out to be a little too cruel for me. I developed a nagging hip irritation, just painful enough to make running frustrating. I needed a substitute. In the summer of 1979 I began swimming in a local lake, sneaking in early before the sunbathers arrived, plodding along at a leisurely crawl for a mile or so. That more than satisfied the urge to exercise; it was also a revelation. That was coming home.

So at age 47 I decided to become an athlete. The pretentiousness of the bald statement makes me wince. I don't think I made that decision as the result of a mid-life crisis. I didn't have a spiritual quest in mind, wasn't suffering from thwarted dreams of glory. I was only going to conduct a modest experiment. I had some ulterior motives.

The training effect is the capacity of the organism to improve itself in response to stress. During the time I was studying the training effect, I was learning everything I could about the body's capacity to get stronger, more effective, more enduring, but over the same period my own physiology was changing in the opposite direction, of course. The little aches, ailments, and insufficiencies of aging had begun to catch my attention.

The physiological downslope of one's life does command a level of attention that isn't quite possible during the upslope, or growth, part of the process. I expected that. Still, I received regular, recurring shocks. Aging is very rude, making no attempt at diplomacy, at softening its message. No small talk: it just starts slamming doors in your face, yanking things out of reach (of your arms, your eyes, your deeper longings).

I claim that I was philosophical about those changes, accepting them with rueful good cheer. I was not applying for membership in the great American youth cult; I did not intend to rage against time. I was interested, however, in giving up any capacity as slowly as possible. I wanted to maintain my faculties at the best possible operating state for the longest possible time, and to give them up, when necessary, as wisely as possible, understanding and acknowledging the process. I had this theory that becoming an athlete would help me do that. My intention was only to conduct a long-term living experiment in how these two contradictory phenomena—the increase from the training effect, the decrease from aging—could be balanced out. That experiment was what I meant by becoming an athlete, and that's all I meant. Oh, sure, said Chris, my wife—and Hitler just wanted a little *Lebensraum* in 1938.

Or maybe I didn't want to be an athlete, maybe I just wanted to pursue some vague idea that I perceived as athleticism. I hate that word, but I can't seem to avoid it. There is no hard definition for it. Barroom arguments erupt over whether racing drivers or jockeys or dancers are in fact athletes. I say they are. I say that dancers are surely athletes, because dancing is hard to do. When any task has a physical component to it, I say athleticism is the quality that helps you do it better—more easily, more surely, more effectively. The size of the movement or the level of effort has little to do with it. In this view violinists, brain surgeons, and carpenters are athletes. I like that idea. There is almost no athletic component to my professional life, but my waking hours are fairly vigorous, and writing is not all the work I do. Part of my interest in athleticism was in order to work better—to get through the physical part of my days more easily, to get more pleasure out of them and less fatigue and discomfort. Age does have a way of making you yearn for improvement in this area.

Besides, it was an amusing idea. I had spent most of my adulthood in flight from the effortful side of life, at least in the sense of hard labor and the dumb-jock image. I've always made my living with my head. The culture I come from values brains over brawn, and it was always clear that whatever I was going to make of myself (interesting coinage, in the physiological sense) was supposed to come about through the products of wit rather than sweat.

As a kid I wanted to be an athlete, of course. (I *was* an athlete; every kid is.) Sports, as another form of play, entertained me endlessly, and I learned them easily and performed reasonably well. By adolescence I was cheerfully obsessed, eager to try anything athletic. Then came the organized sports. I expected formal coaching to open up these new games, reveal their intricacies. More important, I assumed that coaches—adult professionals—would teach me about how to be an athlete, about how to get more performance from my growing body.

None of that happened. The level of coaching available in a small Texas town in the late 1940s effectively killed my en-

thusiasm for physical activity. The organized sports were reduced to rote and drill—and punishment. What passed for
teaching of athletic skills was mostly public humiliation
when we failed. High school sports crammed the dumb-jock
image down my throat. I fled.

And I had been so ripe. I stopped being athletic for reasons
that were as much my own doing as anyone else's, but I did
drift away from that world with the nagging feeling of something left undone. Part of me knew there was something extremely satisfying for me there, if I only knew how to get at
it. Decades would pass before I got around to digging it out,
and then—when I discovered how intricate and beautiful it
was, what rich content it offered—that's when I realized why
I had always hated those coaches so. Those guardians of youth
and pillars of the community had chased me away from
sports. It was almost as if they were trying to protect, rather
than share, the small body of knowledge they were alleged to
possess.

I'm not sure why speed is so seductive. As babies struggle
to learn to stand, they develop the slow-twitch antigravity
muscles; once they've mastered that, they immediately set
out to build up the fast-twitch fibers. As soon as they stand,
they totter, then walk, and then, rising always on tiptoe,
straining upward against gravity, they run. Toddlers toddle
in miniature sprints.

When we were kids we readily agreed that what we wanted
most to experience, in the line of physical sensations, was the
power dive. We were certain that the most horrifyingly wonderful thing you could do was to point the nose of your airplane straight down at the center of the earth and shove the
throttle to the wall. That way you would achieve the maximum speed of the airplane plus whatever additional velocity
gravity could tack on.

As kids we looked for absolutes. We analyzed the physics of the act in those terms: straight down, center of the earth, full throttle, maximum speed *plus*. In those pre-space-flight days, the power dive was as fast as you could go, and we had already decided that speed was an extremely attractive proposition. We were interested in car racing and other forms of rapid travel, but something in us recognized that anything less than this all-out, head-down plunge to earth was kidding around. I mean, if you're going to go fast, why fool around? Power dive.

Eventually the child learns that absolutes won't always serve, that control—a pulling back, a judgmental use of speed and force—works better yet. (I've known children who had trouble getting this point. I may have been one myself.) Until they learn that, however, kids spend a lot of time bouncing off the walls of their own physical limits. I suspect this function is more important than we know. It provides a kind of continuous physical triangulation that helps the child learn to deal with the world more accurately.

By my late forties, I had no more than passing acquaintance with any physical limits except wakefulness, and I think I'd begun to feel a need for some of that kind of triangulation in my life. There has always been something a little bit dogged in my makeup, but I always assumed that anyone could hang on, could try harder, when all you were spending was sweat. That was too easy. I aimed instead for the cerebral life (I wouldn't, on qualitative grounds, call it intellectual), but I never figured out how, in that fuzzy realm, to apply real effort. You can't just *think* harder, or at least I never learned how to do that.

The older I get, the more my efforts to try harder result in Type A behavior, of which heart attacks are made: mere hurrying, pushing against time, which is a lot different from the exhilarating power dive of sheer speed. Sometimes I feel as if

I've been bothered all my professional life by the nagging lack of anything solid to push against.

Physiology provides a metaphor. The proprioceptive organs are those clever sensors buried in our muscles, joints, and tendons that give constant information about body position, direction and rate of movement, and the like. If you don't use the muscles and tendons to make movement, however, the proprioceptors send less information. You start losing your sense of how your body is placed in the world and what it is doing. You have to move (or push against something) to know where you are. It is a metaphor that keeps coming back to me as age tries to limit movement.

So I think that what I was looking for was something to push against. Physiology, again, suggested a solution: how about pushing against the limits to my capacities? I wasn't too sure about the skill component of sports, the gift implied in the phrase "gifted athlete." I didn't think I was even interested in competitive sports, with all their tensions and pressures and heavily freighted victories or defeats.

But the other part of the athletic world has to do with capacity, which is accessible to improvement and which seems directly related to aging. "Athletic capacity" is scientific shorthand for one specific measurement, maximum oxygen uptake. It is the volume of oxygen that the performing athlete can gather and feed to his or her muscle cells at maximum effort, which directly governs how much he or she can do. There are other capacities; I was interested in all of them. My plan was to find out how much I could increase my capacity for physical effort. If a few skills happened to improve in the process, I wasn't going to be miffed. And as for the sports part, well, I'd check that out. There might be something to it that I'd never recognized.

Swimming has always had a powerful attraction for me. I learned to swim when I was six, and for most of the rest of my youth swimming was the only dependable success I knew. Something deep and elemental was touched in me when I learned to trust the water, and I never thereafter missed an opportunity to get into it. I fell for swimming the way little girls fall for horses, and I became pretty good at it.

For the rest of my childhood, any body of water was the first choice of playgrounds. Later, swimming would be associated mostly with ancillary stuff—adolescent summers, courtships, the hormonal rush of growing up—but I never lost touch with the swimming itself. I was a municipal-pool basket boy, a lifeguard, a swimming instructor. I even toured for a little while with a water show, as a clown diver. I guess I was a swimming-pool cowboy. After a year or two of college I began to run out the other end of my obsession, no longer able to justify all the time that swimming pools seemed to consume. Doggedness sets in early. Long before I was old enough for nostalgia, I was sentimental about all that swimming I'd done, all that time so deliciously wasted.

When I began lake swimming in my late forties, I rediscovered a pleasure I'd glimpsed, then lost, nearly thirty years before. In the summer after graduating from high school, I attended a Red Cross water safety instructors' camp—two weeks on Lake Murray in Oklahoma, devoted to intensive drill in all aspects of water safety. The campers, male and female, were in their late teens and early twenties; the counselor/chaperones, not much older, worked hard at keeping us busy from dawn to midnight, mostly in the water. I loved every minute of it.

I also loved a young woman in attendance at the camp, and of course we had a terrible fight, and then I began picking disputes with other personnel as fatigue, testosterone, and immaturity combined their effects over the two-week period. By late afternoon of the last day, I was mad at everybody, and desperate. In violation of everything I'd been taught about safety over the preceding thirteen days, I sneaked down to the dock alone and swam far out into the lake at sunset. In those days I was so romantic I squeaked.

Primitive societies know there is considerable power in rhythmic, repetitive physical action—as in nonstop dancing—to affect the mood, if not to move the consciousness into mysterious regions. That swim certainly did it for me. I suppose I was tired enough and depressed enough to start slowly, at the swimming equivalent of a dog trot. After twenty minutes of steady stroking I found that my irritation with my girlfriend, my fellow campers, and all the rest of the world had dissolved. It was the first time I ever consciously experienced the restful effect of physical work. In those days we didn't dream that just that kind of energy expenditure produces its own tranquilizing hormones.

I don't know how far out I swam, but when I finally stopped and looked around I was a little frightened. I couldn't make out the dock from which I had set out, wasn't even sure I could pick out the camp itself. I turned back because I was a little worried about having the stamina to get back in, but after a few strokes toward shore I started enjoying it again, and I remember feeling the grin on my face as I rolled up for each breath. I took it slow and easy, with a swimming motion so practiced I could put it on automatic. It was an extremely foolish act, and I wanted it to go on forever.

I made it back uneventfully, and slipped in only a little late for dinner. I hadn't been missed. I was not what you would call reticent in those years, but for some reason I told no one where I'd been. My mood was totally changed, and the rest of the evening was end-of-session fun. I really did feel restored.

I didn't think of it then—it never occurred to me until now—but what I'd done was stumble onto a pretty good definition of recreation. There would be moments throughout the next three decades when, in the face of rising tension from one source or another, I would have the quiet sense that what I really wanted was a good long swim somewhere. I never particularly recalled my lake swim at Red Cross camp. I just wished there was some place where I could slip into cool water and set out at a leisurely crawl, and keep it up until I'd reduced myself to a limp dishrag. That particular technique for scratching that particular itch was what I rediscovered in lake swimming twenty-nine years later.

When I was a small child it was the plunge itself, the entry, that thrilled me. (That's why kids spend so much time fooling around diving boards.) As I grew older and a little less hyperactive, it was the swimming part that seized my imagination. I loved being stretched out long and flat in the water, caressed by coolness, using muscle against something that, unlike the recalcitrant world above, gently yielded. Water accepted my efforts; not much else seemed to.

I loved the way the view rolled with my stroke: one moment sun and sky, the next the large blue underwater room where all the physical rules were changed. I loved the bubbling sounds around my ears, the swirl and ebb with which water gives in to and gives back physical effort, the soft quiet of the underwater world. But mostly I came to love making the water work, operating it the way a kid operates a swing or a bicycle. I loved to get a rhythm going, on each arm stroke *driving*, snatching up another surge of forward motion. I loved the wait—the briefest pause, like delaying a step when you're dancing—for the moment in the cycle when the arm pull takes full hold and you can lay into it, using your strength. I loved pouring power into the water and getting motion out, slipping and slithering through it, wriggling away from loss of motion. I even loved feeling it close over me and drag me to a halt.

As I go under the anaesthetic on the operating table, my last conscious image is feathery algae, washing back and forth in a crystal current. It is the deepest blue-green I've ever seen, and I can smell its moistness. I want to bury my face in it. I am swept away from it, into unconsciousness, with an ache of homesickness and loss that makes me weep. I don't know what any of this means, but it has some significant connection with the way I've always felt about swimming.

Three or four years of running had told me that I needed regular cardiovascular work. Swimming could supply that. It was also demanding enough, certainly, to give me something to push against. Okay, I would swim regularly. And then, daydreaming beyond that, it occurred to me that if I were going to swim regularly, I might as well get programmatic (or dogged) about it.

Once before, in an effort to penetrate finally the mysteries of automotive mechanics, I bought a derelict pickup truck, scattered it around my barn, and put it back together. Now I was much more interested in physiology than I'd ever been in truck mechanics. Why not perform the same rescue and reconstruction mission, at least metaphorically, on these 47-year-old bones? Why not see just what I could accomplish, physiologically, with this framework that I'd mostly ignored for the preceding couple of decades?

And while I was at it, why not set myself a proper test, to see how well the project was working out? I'd been studying athletes and athletics for four years from a distance; why not put my body where my brains were? Why not find out what that was really all about?

I once met a research scientist whose field was cosmology. Afterward the friend who had introduced us said, "Just think—what he does is sit and think about the cosmos, and they pay him for that. Isn't this a wonderful society we live in?"

I had much the same reaction—about the wonders of this society—when I first heard about masters competition in sports. Some industrious citizens have gotten together to organize formal athletic competition in several different sports, for every age group right on up to the final decrepitude. Old folks' racing, in other words—although in some of the younger age brackets the level of competition is bordering on the world class. The masters program in swimming is among the most active in the country. Swimmers 25 and older can find competitions ranging all the way from minimeets on Saturday mornings at their local YMCA to well-organized four-day national championships.

Competitors are divided into age groups at five-year intervals. I figured that with three years to go before I turned fifty—the next age bracket—I had plenty of time to get into proper shape. Somewhere off in the future there had to come a moment when the curve of my age and state of condition would intersect with those of the rest of the old geezers engaged in this silliness, and I might start winning races—if I lived long enough. I decided to hunt out that intersection.

But the racing would just be for amusement. The larger motivation—I swore it—was to undertake controlled physical change, and to see what I could come to understand about the biophysical processes involved in these changes. To confront the particle and detail of my own aging, yes, that too—but mostly to confront athletics, to find out what it is that is so fascinating about those individuals who spend so much effort struggling with the complex physical problems of sports.

I never thought it was necessary to break records or win championships to be an athlete. I felt it was only necessary to adopt a certain physiological view, a heightened awareness of the processes by which the body (the athletic plant, rather, which also implies at least some sort of mind) grows, performs, decays, and dies. This is a condescending attitude, implying that athletics are too important to be left to the jocks. I would get cured of that quickly enough.

But it's the attitude I started with. I assumed that the athletic experience was only an intensification of the ordinary life processes. I decided I could stand a little more intensity, at least on the physical side of things. Stand it, hell, I enjoyed it. That was the whole point, wasn't it?

What follows is in small part the story of pursuit of a national championship in one athletic discipline, and in larger part an attempt to set down what I learned in the process about what an athlete is and does. That I happened to choose swimming is of small consequence; what I learned applies about as well to any other sport. Athletics isn't about swimming or running or playing tennis, it's about muscle and nerve endings, about physiology, about certain extraordinary kinds of concentration, about obsession.

That I happened to be of an age not ordinarily associated with such efforts turned out to be fortuitous. I think aging helps you see beyond the swimming or the running to the muscle fiber that makes both possible. It allows you to see these things a little more clearly—and, I think, to experience them more richly. Maybe athletics, like childhood, is wasted on the young.

More important, on the physiological level athletics and aging are opposite sides of the same coin. We don't usually think of aging that way. We think of it as having to do with loss of function, restriction, even mortality. But aging is also about muscle and nerve endings, in what is ultimately a more riveting way than athletics can ever be. When we begin to comprehend it that way, both sides of the coin, aging and athletics, are illuminated. Maybe that's the largest thing I learned. If you look at aging from an athletic viewpoint— from the point of view of their underlying, and common, physiology—both subjects, both experiences, explode with new discoveries. I recommend it.

# THREE

# THE TRAINING EFFECT

S H O R T L Y   A F T E R my forty-seventh birthday I joined
the local YMCA in Northampton, Massachusetts, and made
my first visit to their indoor pool. I hadn't done any physical
work in months and was detrained to the point of creakiness.
Reentry into the damp and echoing world of indoor swimming was nostalgic: clanging lockers, chlorine smells, wet
floors, bored lifeguards. Indoor pools are de facto caverns.
Even the modern ones, lit like operating theaters, feel like
underground chambers; the older ones almost drip with sta-
lactites. The moist, heavy air always soothes. I'd forgotten
how much I enjoyed all that.

After driving through pre-dawn December snows to get to
the pool, cold immersion was the last thing I wanted, but a
hot shower helped me talk myself into it. I found an empty
lane and plunged, holding a long underwater glide, relishing
once more the water's total embrace—just as I used to do
when I was 6 years old. Water, as a medium, hadn't changed
a bit. I am not big on symbolic moments, but the notion did
flit through my mind that with that dive I was starting off on
a strange new course.

The motions of swimming came back quickly enough.
(Needs more *effort*, I thought, after a few strokes up and down

the pool.) I swam a brisk 100 yards, the first fifty of which felt just fine and the last fifty of which fetched me up gasping. Slower, you idiot. (Talking to myself already. It's a peculiar by-product of athletic effort.) I did more laps at a reduced pace, trying to find a rhythm that worked. More distress, but of less intensity. All the other lap swimmers had goggles but I didn't, and I was floundering in a blurry underwater world, groping for the walls at the pool's end. It occurred to me that it might take some time to get on to this activity. I struggled through 800 yards and quit, red-eyed and water-logged.

The next day I managed a slow mile; my shoulders ached, my eyes and ears rebelled, I finished with a headache. I skipped the third day, muttering about being overtrained. The fourth day, with goggles, was easier. (Swim goggles cost about five dollars a pair, and immediately double or triple the yardage you can do without discomfort. Some coaches credit the startling revision of swimming records in the past fifteen years to the widespread adoption of swimming goggles, just because they allow so much more training volume.) For the first time I began to believe I could keep up this regimen.

My plan was simply to swim a minimum distance every session, and keep that up until either the distance grew longer or the task got easier. These were my first halting, ignorant steps along the road to the training effect. I hadn't the foggiest notion what I was in for.

The fitness industry has a problem with the training effect. It is a phenomenon of the physiology, objectively verifiable, right there in hard science, but it is complicated. It just isn't catchy enough for mass marketing. The fitness people fall back on talk of runners' highs, aerobic numbers, positive addiction. The training effect, which is the basic mechanism of fitness—and an immensely more stimulating physiological phenomenon to work with—gets lost in the shuffle.

Seedlings aren't "hardened off" just to withstand cooler temperatures. Plants get leggy when you start them indoors; transplant them outdoors directly and you'll lose some of them, the weak stems snapped by spring breezes. You have to put them out for a few hours at a time, in a sheltered spot, where they can sway in a gentler breeze. That movement sends a message to the stem cells to lay up more lignin, the woody connective tissue in tree trunks. They get stronger. This is the training effect. The training effect is the small, common biological fact that says that if you ask a living organism for more, the organism will, within reason, respond. It is a way of tapping into the cell's capacity for growth. It tends to become the central fact of the athlete's life. To age, on the other hand, is to begin asking the cells for less.

The science part is clear enough. The training effect is a complex series of physiological responses to stress, intricate in detail but marvelously simple in principle. All of training is described in the three phases of Hans Selye's General Adaptation Syndrome to stress: alarm, resistance, and exhaustion. Stress the organism and it reacts, hormonally and otherwise, in alarm, preparing for action: stage one. As the stress continues, the organism marshals its resources to overcome stress and to repair its ravages: stage two. Continue the stress too long and the organism begins to break down: stage three. The training effect takes a multitude of forms, from the laying up of callouses to increasing endurance to forging bodybuilder's muscles, but in every instance the heart of the process is stage two, resistance. It is the stage at which the organism makes internal changes to prepare for a more demanding future.

This concept eluded science, at least in the sense of a unified theory, until well into this century, although athletes have used it, and in fact have understood some of its fine points, throughout recorded history. The principle is certainly plain enough: overload whichever part of the organism you want to improve—overload it *progressively*—and it will develop increased capacity. It is in the application of the principle that complexity develops. That's when the fascination sets in.

As I began to train, all I was suffering from was accumulated disuse. I was putting mild initial stress on my mechanical works, which made for sore muscles, connective tissue, joints. I was also mildly overloading my recovery systems, which meant I was accumulating the products of fatigue faster than I could flush them out, which in turn meant that the soreness lingered a little longer. My bitching about all this was a product of Selye's stage one—alarm.

I seem to have a history of plunging into new activities so hard that one day of work requires two days of rest. I've always had trouble waiting for my body to catch up with its rate of use. I get blisters every time I pick up a hammer, sore muscles from sweeping out the garage. I suspect this kind of unexpected soreness is the initial stimulus behind a lot of sudden bursts of middle-aged athleticism.

The problem is that the consciousness refuses to age. Every middle-aged athlete I talk to insists that there's a 17 year old still inside him or her, the youth who stayed the same while the body it was wearing began to fall apart. (Some say they still see the 17 year old in the mirror.) My sympathy for that complaint grows steadily stronger. My idea of what I should be able to do never changes; the physical plant that has to do the actual work changes every day.

I would prefer not to speculate about the body as separate from the consciousness that guides and perceives it, but my

intellect keeps getting overruled by my gut. Aging accentu-
ates the mind–body split: the unaging consciousness watches
in disbelief as the machinery shudders and begins to break
down. I set out with the fancy idea that I could cure myself of
this split. Training, I thought, would bring the body back
nearer to the capacities it had when I knew it a little better.
Or maybe it would be the aging body that yanked my ideas
back to the physical actuality. In either case, concept and reality would be a closer fit.

Training would, on the best advice, start with the heart. It
is the entry point, the place to insert the wedge to open up the
entire physiology to gain. We think of the heart as the es-
sence of our vitality; we use it as a metaphor for maintenance
of life. In fact we maintain life by metabolizing oxygen in the
cells, and we can stay alive without a functioning heart, as
with heart–lung machines. But the heart works so much better and so much harder than anything else in the physiology—and stops us so abruptly when it fails—that it behooves
us to give it all the help we can. Besides, a detrained heart so
severely limits the amount of effort you can make that there
isn't much choice in the matter of starting points.

The heart is muscle, and you train that muscle as you
would any other, with work. The goal is to increase cardiac
output. Output is the product of the rate at which the heart
pumps, multiplied by the volume of blood pumped in each
stroke. Exercise—effort—just increases heart rate. Training—consistent, repeated exercise—eventually increases
stroke volume. That is, regular exercise stresses the heart,
which responds (stage two, General Adaptation Syndrome)
by growing bigger and stronger, which increases stroke volume. More stroke volume means that the heart pumps more
blood with each stroke, which lets it slow down, which re-

duces the stress. Give the heart some rest by working it harder—the paradox of training. It is a Möbius strip, but you gain a bit on every round.

The formula is simple but the details are complex. Small bonuses keep accruing. Training changes the timing of the heartbeat so that less time is spent in the pumping mode and more time in the refilling—and relaxing—mode. Not only does the trained heart have more time to refill its larger stroke volume, but there is also time for unrestricted blood circulation to the heart muscle itself, which means that muscle is better supplied with oxygen and nutrients, better cleansed of wastes. Over time the trained heart makes specific physical changes—more and larger collateral arteries, increased capacity to dilate the arteries, even increased internal diameter of the coronary artery itself—all of which improve its own blood supply. The standard heart "failure" isn't failure of the heart to continue beating, but failure of the blood supply to the heart tissue. The heart doesn't age, it detrains. It can be retrained.

Training the heart means training that muscle to reach down and grab all the available blood it can, and to eject that blood into the system with a solid, positive thrust. Training teaches the heart to find time to relax momentarily, to take a metaphorical deep breath and set its shoulders for the next beat. It changes the heartbeat from a wispy flutter into a deep and powerful surge. It gives the body a signal—from the heart—that says it's okay to go ahead and work hard. Here, says the trained heart, work with this blood. Plenty more where it comes from.

Or maybe you don't start with the heart, maybe you start with skeletal muscle. Exercise is movement, movement requires muscle, muscle needs oxygen to do its work. "The limiting factor [in physical performance] is not the transport of oxygen to the tissues," says E. C. Frederick, in *The Running Body* (World Publications, 1973), "but the ability of the metabolic machinery to use a high percentage of the oxygen . . . and to sustain that level of utilization for long periods." That ability is developed in the muscle. Start training the muscle, some say, and it pulls everything else along with it. All the other changes—and there are dozens—fall into line.

The interconnectedness of these systems makes any starting point purely arbitrary. The heart can't pump blood it hasn't received, so increased heart rate and stroke volume require an increased rate of return from the veins. To accomplish this, working muscles act as pumps to boost the blood back to the heart. (The veins are fitted with one-way valves to help the muscles pump blood; veins whose valves are failing are called varicose.) There is a similar respiratory pump—the hard breathing of exercise drops the diaphragm, spreads the ribs, expands the lungs, squeezes the blood out of your trunk and back toward your heart. The veins can't return blood that they, in turn, have not received, which means that the processes for exchanging blood in the tissues themselves must also be improved during exercise. Training trains those processes, too.

That's where the training effect starts picking up physiological momentum. Training teaches the muscle cells to deal more efficiently with the materials that are pumped through them. Red cell mass and plasma volume increase. Blood flow and substrate delivery to skeletal muscle increase. Pathways for the processing of these materials are opened up, as training develops new capillary networks (or reopens old ones) and stimulates the growth of the mitochondria—the factories where energy is liberated in the muscles. Mitochondrial enzymes increase. Oxygen extraction is increased. Muscles grow larger not just with muscle-fiber growth but also with increased fluid capacities, increased nutrient content, even increased nerve capacity. And so on, back toward the heart: improvement, growth, increase with every step.

Training even grows bone. As it is with seedlings, so it is with bones: your bones will be just as strong as your life requires. A sedentary life notifies the bone that little strength is required, and the nutrients and building materials for stronger bones are shuttled elsewhere.

Loss of bone density from lack of exercise is called osteoporosis. It begins to happen to orbiting astronauts after even brief periods of weightlessness, freed from the gentle stress (the exercise) of dealing with gravity. Our space explorers carry exercise gadgets onboard, trying to maintain bone density. Osteoporosis also happens to old folks, which is why Aunt Minnie broke her hip. It is not a disease of aging but of inactivity, which literally drains the strength out of the bones. Aunt Minnie sat on her duff too much.

She's also lost a lot of lean tissue. Watch the old folks bob around in the swimming pool down at the Y. As they've gotten older and less active, they've converted their bulk from muscle into fat by not working it hard enough. Their specific gravity plummets as they lose lean tissue. They float like corks. That's an antitraining effect.

These are large physical changes to heart, muscle, and bone, but they actually take place at the cellular level. They are changes that lead to health, but they aren't sufficiently dramatic or sufficiently pleasurable to make fitness converts of anyone. When that conversion does take place, it comes not from subtle physiological changes but from the much larger, pie-in-the-face kind of change: a gross jump in physical capacity that will startle you with your own performance.

The most powerful training effect is on the mind. Once you detect this physical change happening to you, you start finding other results everywhere. The changes give a sharp twist to your perceptual framework. All experience starts getting reinterpreted through this new, positive lens. You get flooded with good news: change is possible.

That doesn't mean it's a piece of cake. I sloshed along conscientiously at my early training, convinced that every additional lap, every increase in yardage, was an act of personal heroism on my part. It took me months to get over that. I spent a lot of time wryly examining the salesmanship of training. The silly thing was how hard I had to sell myself each new increase, each workout. I couldn't do a workout without having to talk myself into it in the first place, and then into each additional piece of work along the way. I dreamed of the day when I wouldn't need to coerce myself each time. It never came. To this day the same stupid argument yammers away in my head through every workout. I don't have to do this, I keep repeating to myself. I can quit any time I want to. I don't think I *can* do this. (Just a little bit more, I answer, and then I can rest.)

Training is . . . training. The only difference between my training and any other is that mine is wetter. It's a block of time taken out of the day and given over to hard physical work. After the pie-in-the-face, breakthrough stage, staying with it is an act of faith. You have to have an eye on the long haul. You can't do it all in one workout, or one week of workouts. Cellular changes take time.

Over the first couple of months I worked my way cheerfully from a slow 1000 yards to a slow mile to a slow 2000 yards—the pie-in-the-face stage—and then, a little less bullishly, to 3000 yards a day, three times a week. Get in, start swimming, count laps. Forty laps per 1000 yards. Try to keep the pace up. Take a break every 500 or 1000 yards—for thirty seconds, or fifteen, or, preferably, ten. Work toward smaller chunks of yardage at a faster pace, and shorter rests, tentatively approaching interval work—like the real swimmers do.

In the beginning 3000 yards took about an hour and a half. The Northampton Y opened at seven a.m., a half-hour drive away. I found myself hurrying into clothes and out of clothes and then back into them again, trying to get through the workout and breakfast and still get to work by about nine in the morning. I couldn't believe I was doing any of this—I'd been a confirmed late sleeper for years—but something was luring me on.

Training's most powerful effect may be organizational. Training regularizes; it gets all systems up to speed, lays out your physiological tools right there on the workbench where you can find them. I began to take great delight in the progression through energy systems as the workout proceeded. During the first twenty or thirty seconds of heavy physical effort, the muscles get their energy from one kind of chemical transaction (anaerobic, not requiring oxygen), for the next couple of minutes from a second chemical transaction (also anaerobic but slightly different), and thereafter from yet a third—aerobic, based on a steady supply of oxygen. Aerobic exercise is simply exercise that you can keep up indefinitely without either tying up your muscles or running out of wind. There are transition stages in which energy sources are combined or overlap.

Different muscle fibers are thought to be used for each stage; different kinds of fatigue are produced. I began to imagine that I could feel each new system kick in—and if that degree of sensitivity was too fanciful, I could definitely feel the difference when, for example, cruising along at a maintainable aerobic rate, I tried to pick up the pace and began to "go under"—into oxygen debt that would eventually drag me to a halt. It was a chance to operate in a new world, my first opportunity to experience some of the stuff the physiology texts were always talking about.

Nevertheless, after a couple of months training began to seem a mighty strange investment. I was setting various goals—projected times for various distances and the like— but not accomplishing them very often. There seemed to be an awful lot of effort invested in small gains. I felt water-logged much of the time. This, I decided, had to be the patience part I'd been warned about.

But the regularization—of my daily life as well as my muscle cells—became extremely attractive. I began to relish the early morning routine, the private time in the water with no interruptions. The investment in time mandated that I get everything else organized—that I plan ahead, get chores done, make good use of the rest of the day. The organizing part began to come easier, and then so did a lot of the other tedious detail of my life. I began to realize a discernible metabolic gain: each day the wick seemed turned a little higher, the biological processing speeded up.

It wasn't that I never got tired. I was spending a gross chunk of energy regularly, which was not without its costs. I developed the decidedly antisocial habit of crashing abruptly in midevening, or even sometimes in midafternoon for a stolen snooze. But I awoke with no hangover of fatigue; sleep spit me out like a cork out of a bottle, full of momentum. Eventually that momentum began to spread into my workouts, which picked up in intensity. I was beginning to get it going.

I started training in early December, then took a break over Christmas and New Year's. Two weeks of traditional ex-

cess, social and otherwise, left me feeling I'd dulled everything from my wits to my sense of touch. My own personal
tradition, repeated every year near the end of that two weeks,
is to begin dreaming of asceticism. I have fantasies about the
monk's cell, scrubbed, spare, cleaned out of . . . stuff. I
dream of fasting, of contemplative minimalism, of Zen-like
singleness of intent. Every now and then, for about ten minutes at a time, I even make an effort in that direction. But the
not-doing of asceticism takes more energy than the doing of
training; reduction, as a strategy, is too negative for my metabolism. I rebound back to excess like a sensory yo-yo. I can
conceive of the ascetic approach only on a short-term basis, as
preparation for more future excess. It won't work. I guess I'm
in this for the long haul after all.

When I resumed training, I was struck by how quickly
flavors and textures picked up their freshness again. It is one
of the more intriguing phenomena of the training effect. A
year or so later another swimmer and I would see it demonstrated more dramatically. We were resting in the shallow
end between sets; it was late in the evening in a local junior-
high pool, and nobody but us swimmers was supposed to be
in the building. "There's a cigarette smoker in the locker
room," the other swimmer said. I sniffed the air and, to my
own surprise, picked up the odor. I went into the locker room
to check. A janitor had started to clean up. He wasn't smok-
ing at the time, but he was a smoker. The same thing happened again from time to time; my teammates and I would
pick up the arrival of a smoker, minutes ahead of time, by the
smell. All that heavy breathing in a moist environment really
cleans out your smeller.

There's a broader physiological rationale for this. My muscles have the power to move me because of chemical reactions

that convert foodstuffs and oxygen into energy. Training improves those chemical reactions. That is, training sharpens and clarifies the very chemical transactions by which energy is generated. You train the muscles to store more energy between bouts of work, to get at and use that energy more efficiently during the work, to replace it more quickly as you recover when the work is over.*

Training trains the cells for *use*, and use improves. What holds true for muscle cells also applies to the various systems that serve and signal the muscle cells. Training cleans the metaphorical palate, sweeping out residue, positioning fresh supplies of possibility. It stimulates, enhances, sweetens the physiology's capacity to respond. Disuse clogs the system; training flushes it clean. Flavors, scents, textures return.

Training will improve my performance not by making me stronger or quicker but by making my cells—muscle, heart, lung, nerve, blood cells—more responsive to the demands I make on them, in the same way that exercise lays down calcium in my bones. Training makes my cells stronger and quicker. It does it by attention to detail. That in doing so it also restores the savor to my salt is just one of training's sweeter bonuses.

Aging, on the other hand, is what dulled the senses in the first place. In *The View from 80* (Viking, 1980), Malcolm Cowley quotes a gerontologist: "Put cotton in your ears and pebbles in your shoes, pull on rubber gloves, smear Vaseline over your glasses, and there you have it: instant aging." Aging does pull a curtain, a thin veil at first, then increasingly thick and muffling layers of insulation. That's one reason for

*This is a capsule version of the entire physiological view of athletics. I never really thought about any of it before I started training; now it colors the way I understand nearly everything in sports.

the disorientation of the aged: all the familiar signals become muted. We have to be able to sense the world to stay comfortable in it.

The senses have a lot of horsepower. (Look at the spice trade, the dye trades, in the Age of Exploration.) So does their diminishment. Their dulling drives me on. What aging takes away—the thing I don't want to let go of—is not so much gross physical capability as it is sensitivity, the availability of acute nerve endings. My senses have given me such vivid pleasure in the past that I am not about to accept their dulling so easily.

When I first launched this nutball project I never considered for a moment that anything even remotely serious was at stake. But it must be that the impulse toward athleticism is not just to fight off the caul of sensory fading but to resist the mortality that such diminishment implies. That makes the remaining time more precious. It makes me more meticulous with the physical side of life; it makes me attentive to finer and finer detail. And that, too, is not a bad definition of the training effect.

# HIGH CAMP

A F T E R   S I X   M O N T H S of working out by myself at the local Y, improving the state of my health but not really making much headway as a swimmer, I realized I was dawdling. I was building up an aerobic base, getting accustomed to a lot of yardage, getting fit but not getting faster. It was time to start working on specifics. I needed coaching.

I needed a good physical exam first, not for any perceived problem but just because the best medical advice says to get one before you start pushing hard. A magazine assignment sent me to Dallas, and the trip gave me the opportunity to have the physical done at Dr. Kenneth Cooper's Aerobics Center in that city. Cooper is the former Air Force officer who virtually invented aerobic exercise as a coherent fitness program; the Aerobic Center's physical exams view the subject a little differently from the way a non–sports-oriented facility would.

Cooper's clinic was crowded when I got there, almost exclusively with middle-aged men who looked fairly prosperous—although before I could check out that socioeconomic observation they took our clothes away and put us into hospital gowns. The lobby was full of graying men sitting around in white smocks with their hairy legs showing, reading magazines and filling out forms. I kept thinking we were outfitted to do the scene where we murder Caesar.

A major part of the physical was the stress test. This treadmill procedure measures cardiovascular function exclusively, in search of hidden heart disease or other symptoms that might preclude heavy exercise. A stress test can't catch every single possibility of trouble, and in fact has been criticized in recent years as an expensive procedure that doesn't catch enough. But it's the best starting point we have for predicting trouble.

The attendant taped electrodes to me in about fourteen places, and started me walking at a good clip—trailing a loom of wires—on the treadmill. After I'd established a stable base, the angle of the treadmill was increased periodically, according to a careful protocol. The attendant also took my blood pressure at regular intervals.

The goal of the test is failure: yours. Your job is to hold off that failure as long as possible. The researcher gets a picture of your heart's performance in the form of a running electrocardiogram, a graphic description of the electrical activity of the heart muscle. He wants to see how your heart behaves under maximum stress. To be sure that the stress has reached a maximum, you continue until you can't go any farther. The most important measurement is how long you last. Other people's spectacular past performances in the stress test were posted on the wall in front of me, on the principle that competitive fire never hurts when you're trying to discover limits. Can I last as long as Roger Staubach did at the same test? (Answer: no.)

I'd always wondered about this peculiar task, with its implication of a precise moment when the organism fails. I knew what it was like to tie up, temporarily, with lactic acid, but I wasn't sure I could really tell when I could go no farther.

It seemed to me that too much psychology was involved. The amount of pure muscular force that subjects can generate has been found to vary by as much as plus or minus 10 percent on any given day. How could that kind of sloppiness be pulled out of something like a stress test? Actually, my unadmitted real concern was that I wouldn't know when to quit. I would either collapse embarrassingly early, from failure of resolution, or out of some misguided hypercompetitiveness I would continue until something awful happened.

I needn't have worried. The first seventeen minutes or so of the test were easy, with the angle of the treadmill low and the exercise still comfortably aerobic. After about twenty minutes, however, things started adding up on me very rapidly. The curve of accumulating fatigue got very steep. I made it to the twenty-fourth minute and knew I was in trouble. The next thirty seconds took about a week and a half, and by the end of that time all doubts about judgment and resolution were erased: I was simply used up. My legs told me that of the total effort that went into the test, about 95 percent had been expended in the last two minutes—and the treadmill angle was just about to be kicked up another 6 percent. I signaled my incipient collapse, made it to twenty-five minutes, and slithered to a stop on legs that felt like wet bread.

I was perfectly pooped, dripping sweat and panting heavily, but I didn't feel *too* awful. There are versions of the stress test that require you to run fairly hard, and they must be tough. Dr. George Sheehan, the cardiologist and running guru, once labored mightily through a stress test, worked himself to an absolute frazzle, sagged gratefully to a nearby cot, and said to the attending doctor, "I have just one question for you. How long until I get to see the baby?"

The stress test results were fine. The rest of the exam was very thorough, from a dental checkup right on through to analysis of stool samples. Percentage of body fat was measured by both the skinfold method (11.4 percent) and total immersion (11.6), designating me "athletic lean." (Normal percentage of body fat for my age and type is 19 percent, "athletic normal" 15 percent or less. Cooper was telling me I was skinny.) My cholesterol was a little high, but so was the HDL—the so-called "good" cholesterol—so the important ratio of these two was okay. My blood pressure could have been a little lower. Everything else was at the good end of the charts. I was a low coronary risk, very low in all but the above. I did lose points as an ex-smoker. (I had quit six years before.)

I am a bad scientist, waiting until six months into my training before the physical, losing my starting point. My stress test put me somewhere between the ninety-fifth and ninety-ninth percentile among 40–49-year olds. This assured me that my suspicions about stress tests were completely unfounded, and pleased me no end. What I didn't know then was that most of the people I would eventually be competing against were easily in the ninety-ninth percentile. That piece of news would have taken a little of the luster off what I chose to regard as a shining performance on the treadmill.

In fact the whole physical exam was a mild medical version of a good news–bad news joke. Good news: my maximum heart rate was 192, nearly twenty points above the predicted figure for my age, which seemed to imply a certain physiological youthfulness. Bad news: I'd *shrunk* half an inch since my height was last measured. Loss of height, from the deterioration of joint materials, is one of the surest indices of aging. The best news was that the treadmill results said I could go ahead, train hard, compete. The bad news was that I had no further excuses. Now I had to do the work.

With a clean bill of (physical) health, I sought coaching. Swim camp seemed to offer the best solution. I'd come across a flyer advertising a camp for masters swimmers, two one-week sessions at a private facility in western New York State. Proprietor John Skehan holds age-group camps for kids most of the summer, but in recent years he's taken two weeks out and invited the old folks. On the Sunday between the sessions he organizes a small masters swim meet.

The more I thought about it, the better it sounded. A full thirty years had passed since I last competed. A swimming camp would be a perfect reentry structure for me, once I got past the jokes about name tags for my underwear and rubber sheets for my bunk. I could get some coaching, and find out what I needed to be doing to rejoin this world of real, if ancient, racers. I would be able to get a week of concentrated training, unlimited yardage in Skehan's fifty-meter outdoor pool*, in a monastic retreat devoted entirely to the sport. They would even throw in a swimming meet for me, so I could find out how you *do* these things. I sent off a deposit.

I drove to "Skwim," as Skehan calls his camp, through a brutal heat wave that made the prospect of seven days in an outdoor pool that much more inviting. Boy, was I going to get a tan. A late-afternoon thunderstorm was gathering overhead as I arrived. The camp was built on a 1900-foot mountaintop in a very hilly area near the Pennsylvania and Ohio borders, plunked down at one edge of a tremendous expanse of short-cropped lawn that looked like a golf course stretch-

---

*Competition swimming pools come in two sizes: short course (twenty-five yards in length), and long course (fifty meters). In masters racing there is a short-course season, climaxing in late spring with a national short-course championship meet, and a long-course season, winding up in late summer with its own national championships. The YMCA also holds its own national short-course championships in the spring.

ing off in the twilight. Quite some distance away from the main bungalow I could just make out the pool, almost in the center of the acres of green. Rudimentary bunkhouses, one for each sex, were set on each side of the clearing, half a mile apart. The whole place was a little surrealistic, but pretty and very wild. I spotted three deer on the way in.

There was cold beer and jug wine available on the dining porch, and before long the assembled adult campers had a small get-acquainted cocktail party going—a hell of a kickoff for my monastic/athletic week. Of the twenty-odd campers in my session there were three or four people who worked with computers, two dentists, two investment brokers, teachers, an editor, some coaches. There was a 34-year-old nun. There were would-be racers in their seventies, but there were also 26 year olds.

We were fed a substantial dinner while the thunderstorm raged, and then introduced to our accommodations—in my case, the boys' bunkhouse, a metal building with a concrete floor. Period. There was a bathroom on one end that had the only electricity in the building. If we wanted to read, it would be by daylight or by flashlight, unless we wanted to sit on a john to do it. Among us middle-aged campers were enough bad backs so that counselors were sent scurrying in search of bed boards for the sagging springs. I found myself speculating about how it was going to be in this barracks when the summer sun started to work on the metal roof and sides. Maybe I could find shade somewhere near the pool for naps. When I wasn't working on my tan.

The swimming pool was available, and some of us strolled over at dusk for an introductory dip. The storm had left the air fresh, the water delightful. It was very liberating to be back in a long, long, fifty-meter pool, and I plodded through a leisurely 1000 meters, relishing every minute of it. Terrific. As darkness fell I began to get a little chilled, and headed back to the bunkhouse. Unfortunately the storm had knocked out the water pump, so I didn't get the hot shower I craved. I crawled into my bunk by flashlight and finally got warm. It was not quite nine o'clock, but nothing seemed to require my attention, so I went to sleep. Another storm rattled through during the night, with thunder and lightning and torrential rains roaring down on the metal roof, but I slept through all but the noisiest parts. It's a talent.

The program featured a "dawn patrol," an unsupervised pre-breakfast swim for anyone who wanted it, but a misty rain was falling and it looked a little raw out there. I passed. After breakfast we met for a more formal introduction, and got a general rundown on schedules and procedures. Skehan, a silver-haired man of impeccable suntan, was director and principal coach, with several phys. ed. graduate students to help. Harry Rawstrom, swimming coach at the University of Delaware and a masters competitor, would be joining us in a day or two. At the pool—in the rain—we were split into groups and assigned coaches, and workouts began.

The daily schedule started with a brief meeting, then a gentle dry-land warm-up—stretching exercises—followed by a morning session in the pool that lasted until lunch. After lunch there was a break—naps optional but almost universal—then a tougher dry-land session, this time working with weights. There were two afternoon swimming sessions: the second was devoted to videotaping, with each swimmer taped individually while a coach commented. While one swimmer was being taped, the rest continued with swimming drills.

I usually managed to sneak another nap before pre-dinner drinks on the dining porch. After dinner it was back to the pool for another session in the long twilight, then a group meeting to review the day's videotapes and discuss stroke techniques and training questions. With the dawn patrol we could get five sessions a day in the pool, along with various other activities. We swam a minimum of 5000 meters a day, and sometimes exceeded 7500. After the first night—and despite as many naps as the day would allow—I never again felt silly about going off to sleep at nine p.m.

Even with five sessions a day the coaches never ran out of new things for us to do. With four competition strokes— freestyle, backstroke, breaststroke, butterfly—there were four different arm strokes to work on, and three different kicks*, with different drills for each. There were technical exercises aimed at improving the efficiency of each stroke, and strength and endurance drills for the muscle systems used in each. There was a minimum of aerobic work (distance stuff) and quite a bit of speed work (intervals at near-sprint pace) in each stroke. There were half a dozen types of novelty drills, aimed at improving the swimmer's feel for the water. There were starts, turns, and finishes, different for the different strokes, all of which have special techniques and key elements that require careful timing. There was the videotape, and time trials. In fact I felt rather distracted by it all—I found myself wanting more concentrated work on fewer elements. But I was exclusively a freestyle swimmer, using the other strokes just for training yardage.

The taping was quite useful. Most evenings you would get to see a couple of laps of your best efforts at one stroke or another, along with a coach's commentary. I've always felt a weird twinge of embarrassment about being filmed in action at anything; one isn't supposed to *care* what one looks like in motion. But to see yourself in vigorous action is always enlightening.

In the first place, you can always spot yourself, even in a

*The freestyle and backstroke kicks are roughly the same.

crowd, no matter how dim the film or brief the action, although you think you don't know beforehand what you look like. And even though you recognize yourself, what you're doing always looks a lot different from what it feels like to be doing it. You usually find you're doing things you not only didn't know you were doing, but would damn well be better off without, to save energy. You don't, in the end, look at such things in order to stylize or prettify your motions, but to simplify them. Which, now that I think of it, should accomplish the same purpose. Anyway, I recommend getting taped. It is a powerful educational tool.

There was one other training tool, an underwater strip of lights on the bottom of the pool that could be lighted up in sequence, to pace a swimmer at any rate of speed the coach dialed up. The lights weren't quite bright enough, so it was useful only at evening session, but it was a fascinating gadget. We would don swim fins and let the light pace us at speeds faster than we could ordinarily swim, to accustom ourselves to moving at materially faster speeds through the water. The lights provide the same focusing effect that the rabbit supplies for racing greyhounds, I suppose. It works.

We were a curious group. I made some particular friends, as I was thrown with some campers more than others in workouts. I fell in with Ron Bryan, an IBM executive in my age group from Washington, D.C., a wry wit who swam endless laps of the exhausting butterfly, trying to rehabilitate a post-surgical shoulder. Donna Burkhart, a.k.a. Sister Donna (or even Coach Sister Donna), was the nun from Seattle, a powerful freestyler who was always in a better mood than anyone else in camp. Dick Guido, a dapper fireplug of an advertising executive from Long Island, swam all the strokes, indefatigably, in preparation for turning 65 and making a serious, national-level run at his new age group. Bob Burns, 32, swimming coach at Choate–Rosemary Hall prep school, a blond giant formerly nationally ranked as a backstroker, argued technique interminably with Skehan. Sixty-six-year-old Don Erion woke us up doing pushups beside his bunk every morning. He owned the best T-shirt in camp. ("U.S. Team, Southeast Asian War Games, 1960–1975. Second Place.")

The campers were all very *nice* people, going about this athletic business with a great deal of modesty—and a lot of groans at every new training task. (Groaning about the work load was the customary technique for establishing rapport.) There was nothing fierce about this group of would-be racers, no discernible fire. Nobody even wanted to admit an interest in competition. I found this a little strange.

These were mature adults who were investing a fair chunk of time and money—and a huge amount of physical effort— to improve at their sport. Yet the unspoken attitude was that the racing part didn't have anything to do with it. All of the talk was about how you do versus yourself, in comparison with your own best efforts. Nobody seemed willing to admit any desire to *win*. Then I realized that I would from time to time see one of these noncompetitors get in the pool and swim 400 meters half a minute faster than he had ever swum before. In the closing laps his shoulders would be knotted, purple with cyanosis, his movements creaking against the semiparalysis of lactic acid buildup. He would be hanging on in grim fury against the failure of his own physical plant. And he—or she—would finish and climb out of the pool smiling, gentled, somehow, by the effort.

Of course I wasn't there to be competitive, I just wanted to learn how to do all that stuff. (Rolling of eyes from Chris.) I did notice that I made sure I got placed in the fastest group of swimmers. I feared getting stuck in a slow group, waiting always for one slowpoke to catch up (as has happened to me in nearly every group ski lesson I've ever taken). Or that was my private rationale, anyway.

It would take me several sessions to learn to curb my own zealousness, to stop straining to be the first to finish every drill, every lap. This was no problem with some of the unfamiliar drills—novelty stuff that I couldn't do properly, that made *me* the slowpoke in the group. But in straight swimming, if there was a body beside me in the water I would try to pass it, as automatically as Pavlov's dog. Fortunately there were swimmers at the camp who could blow my doors off in any stroke at any distance, and who could therefore build my character by humiliating me regularly. They taught me, eventually, to find my own pace.

It rained on the first day, but we swam anyway, popping in and out of the pool, swabbing off with damp towels, standing around in the drizzle to discuss stroke technique. I got cold. By midafternoon I was devising complex heat-retention strategies involving towels and various articles of clothing, all damp. I managed to restore a considerable amount of the lost heat during dinner, but forty-five minutes or so into the after-dinner workout, as we were waiting to swim against the pace lights, I realized that I really didn't want to go back in the water again, and packed it in. You can *do* that when you're an adult at camp.

On the second day of camp it rained, so I passed again on the dawn patrol. There were intermittent showers and brief sunny periods most of the day, with a chill breeze. I shivered a lot. I sneaked off from the after-swim meeting and went to bed early, claiming accumulated fatigue from 10,000 meters of swimming in two days.

The skies cleared on the morning of the third day, and I made the dawn patrol for the first time, getting in a very satisfying 1500 meters before breakfast. This was more like it. Most of us managed to get slightly sunburned by noon, which picked up our spirits. That afternoon the rain returned; we soldiered on through. An evening storm knocked out the hot showers again.

Thursday and Friday were the two heaviest workdays at the camp; it continued to rain, and I continued to freeze. Stroke drills took up the bulk of our days: detailed instruction on the timing of various elements of the stroke, explained with a great deal of hand-waving and elbow-flapping. Swimming coaches speak a private language, with a lot of talk about "squeezing," "pulling," "turnover," "catch"—to describe motions that you almost have to perform to understand. There seemed to be a conscious effort by the coaches to dismantle the strokes that we'd reduced to habit, in order that new subtleties could be introduced. They wanted everything changed slightly, to make us more conscious of what we were doing.

By Friday afternoon I was too cold to concentrate much on the work anyway. I'd taken to hopping out of the pool and into a (damp) sweat suit halfway through nearly every set. I'd wait until I stopped shivering and then go back in; within a couple of laps I would again be knocking paint chips off the pool sides. I just didn't have enough insulation to withstand the recurring drain of body heat. The camp was taking me on a weeklong plunge into hypothermia. It also rained on Saturday, and then on Sunday, which was race day, it rained really hard.

The 1500-meter freestyle was the first race of the day, and we had to seed ourselves, estimating finish times. I had never raced over any distance longer than 200 meters (and that was almost exactly thirty years before). Back in my home pool I'd been trying to achieve a consistent, repeated pace that converted to about 1:37 or 1:38 for 100 meters. A hundred meters every minute and forty seconds would give me a final time of twenty-five minutes flat for the 1500—very neat. So, somewhat recklessly, I entered that time. There were pace clocks at each end of the fifty-meter pool. A minute and forty seconds per 100 meters meant turning a lap every fifty seconds for thirty laps. What could be simpler than that?

(I had never realized how any time-and-distance sport uses these numbers games. It's an arithmetical bureaucracy that becomes the basic currency of training and competition. I worked out for months before I'd learned to do the arithmetic in my head. I still carry a pocket calculator to swim meets.)

I sought out Sister Donna, who, I thought, swam distance freestyle at about the same pace I did. She didn't think she could swim consecutive 100-meter legs at a 1:40 pace, but I talked her into putting down that seed time. We had drawn adjacent lanes, and would be able to pace each other throughout the race. We were set. Some younger campers planned to swim the distance in twenty minutes or so, but we weren't going to let ourselves be distracted by the likes of them.

The start took place in driving rain. I stayed with the field through the first lap—I was once a sprinter, after all, and can go fast if I have to. For a little bit. By the first turn I was in a panic that I was going out much too fast, so I backed off and let everyone go. Everyone went, including Sister Donna, and I was all alone, thrashing away in a dreadful downpour. A lap or so of that and I was in another panic that I was falling too far behind, so I picked up the pace again, at least as much as I could. I was running out of wind almost from the start, which added to my panic: running out of air when your face is

in the water most of the time does not make for a calm and
confident approach. By then I'd lost sight of the clocks, and
had no idea how I was doing for time, place, or moral character.

By 500 meters I was arguing with myself over whether I'd
even bother to finish; by 1000 meters I was sure I was doing
structural damage to myself, and I was still being lapped. I
hung on, swam as fast as I thought I could without perishing,
and wished it were all over with. People kept passing me.
The dismal crush of fatigue was familiar from workouts, but I
never dreamed it could set in as quickly and as sharply as it
did in that race, nor that I could continue to swim despite it.
I swam as hard as I thought was possible. It turned out that
Sister Donna could average 1:40s, but the best I could do
were 1:47s. She beat me by several minutes. I finished sixth
(out of eight lanes). To hell with distance racing.

The sprints went a little better, as my past history indicat-
ed they should: a nervous start, a frantic expenditure of effort
that goes on just a little longer than you think is possible, a
final rush at the wall. I was fifth in the 200-meter freestyle,
second in the 50, third in the 100. There was a special all-
comers' 50-meter freestyle event at the end of the meet, and
in that I slipped to fourth place but cut almost a full second
off my earlier time; thus began the bookkeeping process of
competing with myself. My time for the 100 was six seconds
slower than I'd swum the same event at age 18, which gave
me an interesting morsel to chew on. I didn't get beaten by
anyone over the age of 34, which secretly pleased me—even if
one of the 34 year olds was Sister Donna. Actually, getting
put so cleanly away gave me the perfect summary of the week.
When anyone asked me about camp, I just told them that I
got beaten by a 34-year-old nun, and that pretty well finished
the conversation right there.

When the last race was over we sprinted through the rain

for dryer clothes, then refreshments and post-race chatter in the main cottage. My plan was to sleep over and start home fresh in the morning. As the assembled campers reached the bottom of their beer mugs and began drifting toward dinner, however, Don Erion came over to say good-bye. He was heading down the hill, he said, for a motel room, a martini, a steak, a color TV, and a very long, hot shower. Reentry.

You can do that, too, when you're an adult at camp. Before his car was out of sight I was packing my own gear. I would sort out what the racing was all about tomorrow, when I was warm again. I shook John Skehan's hand, and told him I really would like to stay on for the second week of camp but I'd scheduled some dental surgery, and thought I'd better get home for that. "I don't think I'll use that in the brochure," said the coach.

Two hours later I was sipping a martini of my own. Down in the lowlands it had not rained every day of the past week, and the heat wave had not broken. As I sat over my drink I felt a drop of sweat trickle down the back of my knee, and I smiled.

Rudolf Nureyev was on TV that night, in *Sleeping Beauty*. I watched him in a bleary-eyed stupor of fatigue in my motel room. He was cheating. He was nearing the end of a long number and was beginning to show it—in half-steps, early departures and finishes, movements that didn't quite hit the mark (but then were allowed to drift, slyly, into place). It wasn't glaring; he was too masterful for that. It was only that his performance had gone a little soft. His crispness, his accuracy, was slipping away at the end.

Oh, how I had cheated in the 1500. Swimming takes place in a languid and restricting medium, and so the search for efficiency becomes paramount. Swimming technique is aimed not only at producing a powerful driving force through the water but also at conserving the momentum that results. The swimmer must concentrate on reducing drag as well as on generating speed. One place he or she can do this, for example, is on the turns. When you push off from the pool wall the glide not only gives you a burst of speed, it also gives you a brief rest. To get the most from the glide, however, you must reduce drag to a minimum. You stretch your arms over your head, point your toes, and pull, *hard*, elongating yourself into as thin and streamlined an object as possible. There are twenty-eight turns in the 1500; working the turns hard can make half a second's difference on every one of them.

But the elongating stretch takes energy just when you want to rest, and as you get tired, that hard pull will be the first thing to go. When it does, you start losing speed and distance on your glide, so you have to start stroking earlier. In the end letting up on the glide costs more energy than it saves. I knew this, but when I got tired I did let up. Just this once, I would tell myself, just for the next turn, I really don't want to come up with the effort again. And I kept on saying that, turn after turn.

It is a small example, but it stands for the larger problem. In the leaden last laps of the 1500 I came up with a catalog of drag-producing small errors generated out of fatigue. As I struggled for more air, my stroke developed a lope—a surge and subsidence. (It's the subsidence that kills you; you have to get the momentum back, and that takes effort.) I dropped my elbows, losing the pulling surface area of my forearms. I chopped my stroke short, yanking my arms out too early. It felt terribly sloppy and lazy to swim that way, and yet it was taking all the energy I had.

Maybe, I began to think, the athlete's job—the performer's job—is just to preserve the crispness, to push the precise and efficient motion on through to the end of the task. I wasn't sure whether you do this by means of physical conditioning alone, or with a kind of mental discipline that just won't allow the sloughing off of technique to take place. I was fairly sure I would find out that you do it with both, along with any other schemes, strategies, and preparations you can find to throw up against the problem.

I'm sure that near the end of a long performance, Nureyev also doesn't feel crisp anymore. I'm sure that he was telling himself, near the end of this performance, that (just this once) he really didn't want to come up with the effort to nail that next *entrechat*. It showed, this time; it usually doesn't. That for so very long he has always nailed the next *entrechat* is a part of his greatness.

And this isn't the only way to distinguish me from Nureyev, either.

There are other adult sports camps available, particularly for tennis and running. Recently there's been considerable publicity about adult camps in baseball, football, basketball (at roughly twenty times the 1980 cost of my swim camp, which was $150). As the masters movement and other middle-aged sports continue to grow, other disciplines will surely adopt the camp concept. Ski resorts have been holding them for years, calling them "ski weeks." I've attended ski weeks (and managed to stay warmer at some of them than I did at swim camp). The general atmosphere is much the same, although ski instructors are more accustomed to working with adults than are swimming coaches.

It is the concentrated experience that adult campers are after, of course, particularly at the entry level. It works. I certainly got my money's worth. I came away from Skwim's racing camp with my technique sharpened, with my head crammed full of new ideas, and my body (once I got it warmed up again) eager for more work. I got started racing again, and learned that I needed a great deal more experience at it. I learned I really wasn't in nearly as good shape as I thought, no matter what Dr. Cooper's numbers had said. I still had my work cut out for me.

# FIVE

# DO NOT PITY THE
# AGING ATHLETE

"The traditional Eskimo remains extremely fit and active until his son has become a skilled hunter; thereafter, he has the privilege of choosing the best items from the game won by his son, and his physical condition shows a rapid deterioration."

—Roy J. Shephard, M.D.
*Physical Activity and Aging*

D R.  M I C H A E L  P O L L O C K is director of the Center for Evaluation of Human Performance at Mount Sinai Medical Center in Milwaukee. For the past dozen years he has been conducting a longitudinal study for which he recruited twenty-four athletes, all of them regional or national champions, many of them world-record holders. He first tested them in 1971; when I interviewed him, he was in the midst of running them through a tenth-anniversary battery of measurements. This group of world-class athletes ranges in age from 50 to 82, and all are still training. Eleven of them still compete at high levels.

Pollock's study collects the standard measurements of exercise physiology: percentage of body fat, lean body mass, lung capacity, blood pressure at various levels of stress, resting and maximum heart rates. And VO2 max, of course—

maximum oxygen uptake, the maximum rate at which oxygen can be consumed.

(VO2 max is the best single measure of the capacity of the aerobic system. It is usually expressed in milliliters of oxygen per kilogram of body weight per minute—ml/kg/min. Untrained males aged 20 to 29 have VO2 max values on the order of 40–45 ml/kg/min. World-class marathoners may achieve 70–75; there are cross-country ski racers who have been measured as high as 88.)

The textbooks tell us that VO2 max declines about 1 percent per year. Some texts claim that training can reduce that decline to 0.5 percent, or about 5 percent per decade. Some of Pollock's subjects have maintained virtually the same VO2 max over the ten years of the study—or have improved.

An earlier study by Pollock showed that athletes who continued training remained fairly stable in these measurements through their fifties and up to about age 60, then dropped off radically from age 60 to 70. "But," Pollock told me, "our sample in the original study had only three athletes at age seventy, and they weren't training all that much. Their training had dropped off dramatically."

The new study draws on a larger sample. Not all of the current subjects have maintained their intensity of training over the ten-year period—nearly all have had periodic dropouts from injuries or other reasons—but, in general, total training volume has stayed the same. While the overall statistical picture again shows decline in the usual measurements with age, the changes are not linear.

"It had been established that the aging process is linear," Pollock says. "But this study shows that when people continue to train at the same level, they seem to be able to hold on. The marked drop-off that we got in the earlier study didn't show up this time, particularly in the ones who continued to train hard.

"The aging process isn't linear, it's curvilinear. There's a bend in there somewhere, but it's not just a downslope right from the start. There are some plateaus. The plateau we found, among people who trained hard and were heavy competitors, was with the group up through age 55 to 60. After that it seems to bend downward, but even after the curve starts down, there's a measurable difference between subjects based on how much training they're doing."

Nobody knows what aging *is*. The American Medical Association's committee on aging studied it for over ten years, and didn't find one physical or mental condition that could be directly attributed to the passage of time. Theories abound, of course. Some theorists propose a genetic clock. Human cell cultures will divide about fifty times and then, unaccountably, they die. Young cells frozen after twenty divisions, then thawed, take up where they left off, dividing thirty more times before dying out. The implication is that something in the cell is keeping count.

Other theories have to do with error—accumulations of genetic damage from radiation or other sources that gradually destroy the cell's ability to repair itself, or to replicate accurately. Recent research focuses on the autoimmune system, which is linked to the thymus gland. The thymus shrinks with age, and so does the system's ability to fight off infections and to recognize foreign material in the system.

Laboratory animals have been found to live longer if their food intake is sharply restricted in the first half of their lives; fish live longer if the temperature of their environment is reduced in the second half of their lives. This begins to sound like the old joke: when you're that hungry or that cold, maybe your life just seems to last longer. The popular press continues to announce another new theory of aging every few weeks. None quite identifies what the phenomenon is.

We all recognize aging, in the thinning gray hair, the wrinkled and sagging skin, the stooped posture of our elders—and in the onset of these signals in ourselves. But there is no overarching theory that ties these universal signals together with a single explanation that we can call aging.

Cellular and molecular theories of aging are ultimately concerned with life span itself, which has not been budged from the biblical three score and ten despite the wonders of modern medical science. Most of us active citizens, athletic or otherwise, are perhaps less interested in mere longevity than we are in function. What we want is the maintenance of full function beyond the years of youthful vigor.

What we get is deterioration. Here's what science tells us to expect from aging. We not only lose about three quarters of an inch in height per decade after age 50, we also lose sitting height, shoulder width, and chest depth (but our ears and noses grow larger, and even our hat sizes increase). We finally stop gaining weight at about age 55, and thereafter slowly lose it. But we may look fatter than ever: all we're doing is converting lean muscle into fat. We lose not only minerals from our bones but some of the matrix that holds the minerals in place.

We begin to lose lung function. Weakening shoulder and back muscles pull our upper bodies inexorably forward and down, into the traditional humpbacked appearance of the elderly. With the curved back comes a general loss of joint mobility—where the ribs meet the spine and the breastbone, for instance—which reduces rib-cage elasticity. These structural changes, plus wasting of respiratory muscles, make breathing more work. The biochemical processes for getting oxygen to the tissues don't deteriorate too badly; the loss of efficiency is in the mechanics of breathing.

A greater loss of function comes from aging's effect on the

heart. "There is a striking parallelism between the effects of older age and cardiac disease," say Dr. Raymond Harris and Lawrence J. Frankel, in *Guide to Fitness After 50* (Plenum Press, 1977). As we get older we reach peak cardiac output at a lower work load. Our maximum heart rate goes down. To maintain a given level of effort, each part of the cardiorespiratory system has to function closer to its maximum, which leaves us less reserve. When we're operating that close to maximum, fatigue sets in earlier. Cardiac output in general decreases about 1 percent per year, very likely from loss of muscle power in the heart itself. Wastage is general: each decade, we actually lose some 3 to 5 percent of our metabolically active tissue.

Muscles shorten. As they do, they cause skeletal changes that can impinge on blood flow, decreasing oxygen supplies not only to the muscles (further taxing cardiac output) but also to the brain (taxing our patience). Motor responses grow faulty, decreasing our coordination and physical stability. There is a slowing of the tonic neck reflexes and other feedback mechanisms that help us retain balance, fight off vertigo, judge movements. We grow clumsy. If injured, we heal more slowly. Our ability to adjust to any change grows poorer.

But mostly, aging dries us up. It is loss of fluid in the lens of the eye, for example, that stiffens it, making it less able to adjust to different focal lengths, driving us to bifocals. Aging's loss of height is caused by the drying up of the lubricants that keep cartilage and joint surfaces thick and healthy. In fact it is this drying up, this loss of elasticity in the connective tissue that holds us together, that is the single most characteristic physical change from aging. It is almost as if the cells themselves begin to lose their moist liveliness, their drying membranes setting up fibrous barriers to the easy transactions of healthy metabolism. Youth *is* juicy; age is sere.

The shortening of muscles is caused by changes in connective tissue. The cells of connective tissue contain elastin and collagen. Elastin provides the elasticity; it is fifteen times more elastic than collagen. Collagen provides the strength; it is twenty-five times stronger than elastin. Age changes both. The elastin frays, its fibers fragmenting; the collagen increases in density and stability, drawing tight the network of connection, changing the way our parts relate to each other. "Back and joint problems, tendon ruptures and altered pressure–volume relationships for the lungs, heart, and great vessels can all be traced at least in part to disturbances of connective tissue," says Dr. Roy J. Shephard, in *Physical Activity and Aging* (London: Croom Helms, 1978). I keep thinking of those fishnet shopping bags of which the French are so fond.

"Speaking generally, all parts of the body which have a function, if used in moderation and exercised in labors to which each is accustomed, become thereby healthy and well-developed, and age slowly; but if unused and left idle, they become liable to disease, defective in growth, and age quickly."        —Hippocrates (460–377 B.C.)

That is, these are effects of aging if you don't exercise. Harris and Frankel describe aging's effects in the brain and central nervous system, for instance, as changes that "impair sensory perception and motor responses so that . . . coordination, motivation, ability and desire to exercise lessen and the simple, effortless responses of youth become slower and more labored in later life." Pretty damned depressing. But they continue: "Formerly, it was believed that these [slower reaction] times were strictly a function of age, but recent evidence suggests that they may also be a function of an individual's psychological or physical fitness level."

That last sentence has a way of becoming the theme song of aging research. In the most carefully designed scientific test, it is virtually impossible to discriminate between the effects of aging and the effects of inactivity. Scientists can't really test the elderly because the elderly aren't fit enough to be tested. Researchers run up against weaknesses, deterioration, incipient pathologies that preclude their obtaining solid data. When the elderly *are* fit—see Pollock's study, and others—the phenomenon more or less disappears. They aren't elderly anymore.

I'm exaggerating. Perhaps I am mixing categories. Perhaps when investigating aging, we should restrict ourselves to questions of longevity, and to those cellular and molecular considerations. When we are investigating loss of function, we should discount aging, and only consider what Dr. Hans Kraus calls hypokinetic disease—the ailments and disorders that are *caused* by lack of movement, by underuse.

There is documented evidence for this, too: "It can generally be concluded that morphological age changes are preceded by functional limitation in the corresponding organ. The aging process, especially the functional involution of the organism and/or special organ is, therefore, not a simple consequence of morphological loss or morphological changes of tissue. On the contrary, *the functional involution is a primary process and the morphological involution is a secondary one*, probably a consequence of the former. [Emphasis added.] Aging, therefore, represents a process of tissue change which can be postponed by preserving the functional capacity of organs and organisms on an adequate level."* Or, use it or lose it, just as Hippocrates told us over 2000 years ago.

*From a chapter in Harris and Frankel entitled "A Follow-up Study of the Effect of Physical Activity on the Decline of Working Capacity and Maximal O2 Consumption in the Senescent Male," by Fischer and Parizkova.

I used to be agile. Few of aging's other physical notifications have struck me more sharply. (Other middle-agers have told me of the same loss.) I really miss agility. I used to teach trampoline, perform as a diver, tumble on gym mats. I loved to trot along dry creek beds, leaping from boulder to boulder. I never fractured a single ankle. Now I wouldn't try it for all the orthopedists in Aspen.

The onset of clumsiness in my forties was one more significant stimulus to get back in shape. I'd begun to have this weird feeling that I no longer inhabited my own full dimensions. It was as if I didn't know exactly where my limbs were going when I moved them, how far I could reach, where my physical boundaries were. Sure enough, one of the most immediate benefits of training was the fine, loose feeling of inhabiting my full self again, all the way out to the edges.

As training has continued, I've necessarily changed routines from time to time. Each time I do, I go through another period of distortion and readjustment. I may feel larger or smaller, lighter or heavier than I'm used to. I always discounted this as imagination. There are vaguely analogous findings in the literature—changing self-perception with exercise and the like—but they sounded too subjective to carry much weight.

Recently others have been telling me of the same reaction. Steve Kiesling, a former Olympic rower, takes a new job and must drastically change his training practices: "I feel all the wrong size," he says. A young woman starts a Nautilus program, loves it for a while, then quits: "It makes me feel *bigger*, and that's the last thing I want." They are getting unfamiliar readings of their own dimensions.

There is physiology for this, too, and it is related directly to disuse. "Habitually sedentary elderly subjects suffer not only muscular deterioration, but also distortion of body image," Harris and Frankel say. "They perceive their bodies as broader and heavier and body activities as more strenuous than they actually are." Feedback between movement and body image goes awry, and the less the individual moves, the greater the change in body image. The result is growing clumsiness, increased fear of physical activity. "Older people lose the pleasure of movement simply for the sake of moving, which children enjoy. They eventually become reluctant to move at all, and may opt to remain in a chair or bed."

Movement itself will reverse these distorted self-images. This leads Harris and Frankel to speculate about the psychology of disuse: "Muscular movements initiate stimuli in muscle spindles which are essential for optimal functioning of the central nervous system. There appears to be a relationship between an individual's mood and his muscle condition and posture. The gamma motor system appears involved in this relationship. [The gamma motor system is a feedback servomechanism that operates through the muscle spindles and helps coordinate movement.] Any feeling of happiness, alertness or attention may increase the gamma motor system activity. Unhappiness, drowsiness, or lack of attention may decrease the activity in these fibers." The more I learn about proprioception—"self-sensing"—the more enraptured I become with the gadgets that do the work. Here is one direct, physical way that exercise makes you feel better.

Muscle spindles are proprioceptors that measure length, change of length, and rate of change of length in the muscle. The muscle spindle is composed of two kinds of muscle fibers gathered into a bundle. Both types of fibers are capable of being contracted, and also of sending signals to the central nervous system. The gamma system is the neural loop connecting one kind of fiber with the other, by way of the central nervous system.

When both fibers are the same length, as in gentle, accustomed activity, all is quiet. When the difference in length is increased—when you start using the whole muscle in hard contractions, or stretch it out—both kinds of fiber send signals through the gamma loop system. The signals try to bring the two sets of fibers back to comparable length, which is part of the stretch reflex. They also send signals that make you aware of the change. One of the two types of fibers provides the power, quickness, and gross movement in muscular contractions. This type, called extrafusal, makes up the bulk of the muscle. The other type, called intrafusal, is used for fine control, for delicate small adjustments.

At the first level of function, then, the gamma system helps you control movement more accurately. At the next level, operating as a kind of depth gauge, it is the system that tells you what your dimensions are up to, where your edges are. It is the system that keeps you located and measured and in accurate physical relationship to the world.

When you undertake unusual activity, the gamma system sends you unusual information, which distorts your self-perception until the new wears off. In the case of the elderly, the bedridden, the grossly inactive, lack of regular use of the gamma system causes them in effect to lose track of themselves physically. We've traditionally considered this loss an inevitable result of growing older. It's from disuse.

The gamma system maintains muscle tone, the underlying, low-grade contraction that literally keeps the muscle alive. (Snip the gamma loop and the muscle it innervates will atrophy like a paraplegic's calves and thighs.) Muscle tone maintains our antigravity muscles. These are the muscles that not only make your legs capable of holding you erect, but—in hips, back, stomach, shoulders, and especially in the neck and head—make you into a biped. It is musculature that you began putting under automatic control on the day your mother first propped you into a sitting position, a system that you've been able virtually to ignore since early in your second year. The antigravity muscles literally and specifically determine your posture. They determine your "attitude"—which term can also refer to your emotional approach to the world. Suddenly physiology begins melting into psychology.

The scientists say that happiness, alertness, and similar emotional states may increase gamma system activity, and that unhappiness may decrease its activity. For some reason they are reluctant to say that increasing gamma system activity (which can be done deliberately with exercise) will increase happiness, alertness, and the like. Feeling good, which requires exercise, is still too much trouble.

One of aging's most powerful physical effects seems to be the shrinking, dwindling, loss of range of motion, stiffness, malfunction of joints, reduced stature, and other related connective-tissue ailments, for which the only antidote I've been able to find is movement—exercise, and stretching. A concomitant problem of aging (seldom considered physiological) is depression, dulling, the dwindling away of emotional tone in a way that is a perfect psychological analogy to loss of muscle tone, to diminished range of motion. The gamma system is where these two sets of symptoms meet.

Range of motion is the perfect metaphor, because here is how age finally gets you: it reels you in. The mechanism is so clear it's unnerving. I recently observed a not terribly active 75 year old who spent three weeks in bed with a very sore back. Tests have demonstrated that three weeks of bed rest will decondition even the best-trained young athletes. We don't think very much in terms of deconditioning when it comes to inactive 75 year olds, but that's exactly what it did to my friend. It was as if she were tumbled forward—in age—at an accelerated rate.

Once she was up and about again, it was clear that she had converted a lot of lean muscle mass into fat. (She gained no weight, did increase in bulk, lost a great deal of muscular strength.) She didn't feel like doing much, and when she did, she suffered from shortness of breath, dizziness, and general fatigue, all of which discouraged her from attempting to do more. It discouraged her from doing what she needed to do to regain what she'd lost. In short, she came back slowly, and didn't come back all the way. Her *range*—from the distance she could walk to how far she could reach to the very nature of the aims and ideas she was willing to entertain—was noticeably shortened. Nature was pulling in the string. Another illness, an injury, a reduction of activity of any sort, will pull the tether shorter yet.

Age is clever that way. It is not that it pulls so hard, but that it is so vigilant. It is very patient, having more time than you do. It monitors you. Allow any slack—anywhere—and age, like a spider, will snatch it up and bind it in place with newly rigid, inelastic connective tissue.

Dr. Pollock's aging athletes are keeping the string taut. The ones who show no significant deterioration from aging are the ones who have the perseverance, the motivation, the courage (and the genetic equipment, and the good fortune) to keep the string a whole lot tauter than the rest of the population.

Consider the case of Hal Higdon. Higdon is one of the wisest and most prolific writers in the field of fitness, a contributing editor to *The Runner*, author of *Fitness After Forty* and several other books—and a bona fide world-class athlete.

He ran a 2:40 marathon in 1971 at age 41, which was pretty good; he ran a *2:29* marathon in 1981, a few months short of his fiftieth birthday (and won a world championship, at the top of his age group, in the process). When he was 41 he entered the ten-kilometer race in the national championships and took fifth place outright, irrespective of age groups, against Olympic-caliber youths. He has been tested three times by Pollock, in 1971, 1976, and 1981.

The significant measurements:

|  | 1971 | 1976 | 1981 |
|---|---|---|---|
| Max VO2 (ml/kg/min) | 62.7 | 62.7 | 63.2 |
| Max heart rate | 160 | 160 | 160 |
| Resting heart rate | 34 | 32 | 33 |
| Percentage of body fat | 10.9 | 9.5 | 10.3 |

*Blood pressure remained the same; lung capacity remained the same or increased slightly.*

Higdon was doing a great deal of training on the track in 1976, in preparation for some large event or other, and says that the higher intensity of that work explains the slightly better readings for that year. But it is clear that as far as the physiological measurements are concerned, in the past ten years, Hal hasn't aged, he's "youthed." He says he's been able to maintain or improve these figures only because he trains more intelligently as he gets older, and as a result loses less training time to injury.

Pollock's study is continuing, and so are his athletes. The accumulating figures are gradually building a picture that shows a percentage change downward with age in physical measurements—a few points different, one way or the other, from the results shown by similar but less extensive research projects. This is not to denigrate Pollock's study. Those few points of change are extremely significant in science. The greater span of years involved, the larger sample, the care and precision with which the data are gathered and analyzed, will provide more clues to unlock the puzzle of aging, and we'll all be richer for the accumulation of knowledge.

But the Hal Higdons and other aging athletes out there who persevere won't fit the curve. The percentages will go down—perhaps because of the effects of aging, perhaps because of the injuries and failures of motivation and the general watering down of quality that sheer numbers inevitably bring. Numbers are what science is all about. The individuals who persevere will maintain. Individuals are what athletics are all about.

Pollock says his study will show that intensity of training affects physiological measurements more than sheer mileage does; that high-level performers maintain aerobic and performance capacities better than those who train with less intensity; that reductions in performance values are not related to age in a directly linear way—in masters athletes who continue to train. It will also show that age appears to affect performance (as in actual times posted in competition) more than it affects physiological function (as measured by standard tests). Among aging athletes, actual performance does not hold up as well as physiological function does. In the older athlete, performance declines faster than the other measurements do; in the best older athletes, performance declines even when the other measurements stay the same. This is frustrating as hell to competitive oldsters, of course. But do not pity the aging athletes: all they are giving up is performance. They are hanging on to all the rest. What they're doing is keeping the string pulled taut.

This is dangerous thinking. Beware the zealot. My eyesight alone tells me that plenty of aspects of aging are irreversible. Scientists caution against these grand expectations from so diverse and vague a collection of processes. They can demonstrate in their labs only small fractions of these processes, a barely significant percentage of gain in body chemistry here, a minuscule improvement in heart function there. They will, however, admit that all such improvements do seem to be interrelated, as any change in bodily functions spreads ramifications through the rest like ripples from a tossed stone.

The physicists tell us that the universe is running down, that over time all matter is inevitably degraded to an ultimate state of inert uniformity in the process known as entropy. I prefer the view of Nobel laureate biologist Albert Szent-Györgyi, who proposes that living matter is syntropic. The very use of living tissue, says Szent-Györgyi, stimulates growth and development, and increases the tissues' own ability to resist future stress. He's talking about the training effect.

BOOK
TWO
THE WORK

# SIX

# WHY WORKOUTS ARE THE WAY THEY ARE

Y O U C A N ' T D O A S well training by yourself, they say. I resisted that thinking for a long time. Obviously you could do the work—put in the distance, maintain your times. You might be giving up a little camaraderie, a little moral support, but the point was the amount of work, wasn't it? Besides, when I was running, one of the things I enjoyed most was the private time, alone.

Swim camp had convinced me, however, that I needed to find a better pool. I'd been swimming at the Northampton Y, which was usually crowded and always too warm. (Hard swimming works up a sweat. It's very unpleasant in a pool that's too warm.) When I heard there was a masters group working out at the local junior high in Amherst—about the same distance away in another direction—I looked them up. Their pool was cool, fast, and uncrowded. I signed on, becoming a permanent member of the little group known as the Valley Swim Club. We had a "coach"—a qualified lifeguard who would occasionally give us a suggestion about workouts. There were roughly a dozen regulars, only a couple of whom were much interested in competition. The rest were fitness swimmers.

They were a cheery bunch, though, and I swam through

the winter with them. Spring came, and our lifeguard was replaced by a young man named Bill Tyler, who was finishing up his bachelor's degree that summer. He had been an exceptional high school swimmer, had swum in college, and thus was a fresh product of an active program. He started out just lifeguarding, but he got interested in us, and became a real coach for our little group. Before long he had figured out exactly how to push all my buttons, and I began to find out what a proper swimming program might be like. He had more to do with making me a racer than I can possibly explain.

A couple of months after Bill began coaching us, there came a night when I would get a workout with three other swimmers at about my own level, the four of us within a second of each other over 100 yards. We had to share a single lane, "swimming in circles"—keeping to the right to avoid oncoming traffic—to save space. (This is standard practice for age-group kids and school swim teams, but I avoid it when I can.) He then gave us a crushingly difficult workout.

We set out at five-second intervals. Immediately we were each swimming in the wake of the swimmer ahead, aswirl in a froth of bubbles, with someone else coming along behind at the same or faster pace. It was difficult to start with, but it required such madhouse scrambling to keep up that the fatigue got put aside, ignored, in order not to break the rhythm.

It wasn't that any of us was trying to beat anyone else. There wasn't any sense of a contest to it. But there was always the tantalizing possibility that with each stroke you just might touch the fluttering toes of the guy ahead, which would provide a funny little stimulus to the exercise. And the fellow behind might at any moment tag *you*, letting you know you were dragging down the pace, which did tend to keep you squirming along, trying to eke out another inch or two of space.

We finished the set on time and started another, only a little less grinding. We finished that and Bill started us doing head-to-head time trials. I thought I was absolutely used up after the first set, but I made it through the second, and held my own in the time trials. By the time we finished, the workout totaled about half again as much work as I'd ever been able to get through in a single session, almost all of it accomplished in near-panic, grabbing and yanking at the water any way I could, all form and dignity abandoned. When it was over we had done things that I couldn't do.

I would never get another workout quite like that one, and I didn't think I would miss it, but it stayed with me for weeks. I kept remembering it, and when I did, the thing that characterized it most clearly—through the fog of fatigue— was how much fun it had been. I hadn't thought of it that way at the time. I was either digging in, trying to touch the next guy's toes, or I was hanging on the wall with my tongue out, wondering if I was going to perish. But I remembered it afterward as hard-nosed, exuberant fun that held me on the verge of laughter the whole time. It was childlike. What it really reminded me of was a good game of kick-the-can when we were kids.

"Dignity abandoned" says a significant and subtle thing about training, I think. When you finally begin to train hard, you discover you can't carry the excess baggage of reserve through the process. I never think of myself as clinging to attitudes, stances, personal dignities, but of course I do. They are curiously related to noncommitment. It is only in the frantic effort of an extremely hard workout—or an athletic contest—that I find myself tossing all that out, abandon-

ing the reserve that keeps me from bringing maximum effort
to the task. When I do, the feeling is always childlike. That
may be one of the largest appeals of athletic competition. It
pushes you out of your own stiff reserve, back into the non-
judgmental commitment of childhood. It is a joyful and vul-
nerable place to be.

I don't know why you get a synergistic gain from other
swimmers. I've had just enough of a taste of it now—reaching through the bubbles for the next guy's toes, swimming
faster, for longer, than I thought I could—to know that it
happens. It's real. It may not be just muscle fibers, but I
doubt that it is plugging into each other's aura or force field
or any of that West Coast stuff.

Still, if you put living heart-muscle cells in a Petri dish,
they will continue to contract in a regular rhythmic beat.
And if you take two of them that are beating at different intervals and put them in the same dish together, before long
they will be beating in perfect synchronicity.

I slither into a nylon wisp of a swimsuit, grab my equipment bag, and join the other swimmers at poolside, gathered
around the posted workout:

```
Warm-up: 3 × 200 KPS .............. 600
5 × 100 on 1:30........................ 500
1 × 500 on 6:30........................ 500
5 × 200 on 3:00 Desc ................1000
8 × 50 on 2:00 ......................... 400
200 Swim-Down ......................  200
                                    3200
```

Over my shoulder somebody groans, pointing at the 5 ×
200. Looks tough. We yawn, flex creaky joints, put off get-

ting wet. Might as well get it started. I splash water on my face, don goggles and cap, dive in, wincing slightly at the coolness. Here we go again, I always say to myself. I glide to the surface and begin a slow first lap, checking out the state of my shoulder joints, feeling around for a workable rhythm. I roll into the first turn, push off, glide, and begin picking up the stroke rate, putting a little force into my pull. I'll swim a 200 first, I decide—eight laps of freestyle—and then do the kicking and pulling.

### *Warm-up: 3 × 200 KPS*

The line that says "3 × 200 KPS" means we're to do two hundred yards each of kicking, pulling, and swimming, at our own pace. "On 1:30" and other times on the lines that follow mean that we must start the next segment one minute and thirty seconds after starting the first. Kicking is doing laps using leg power alone, hanging onto a float. Pulling is arms only, a float between your legs. Warm-up time is usually divided among these exercises plus the various strokes. Tonight's workout is all freestyle.

Every workout starts with a warm-up, a few hundred yards set aside for getting all physical systems up to speed. You are literally raising the temperature, and thus the resiliency and flexibility, of the flesh. You are also raising your heart rate, which stimulates circulation, which begins to deliver more energy to, and carry more wastes from, the flesh that is doing the work. You're cranking up the factory for a spell of full production.

When I was younger I wouldn't take the time to warm up for anything; the older I get, the more carefully I try to prepare for effort. Still, I never know until I'm in the water what sort of warm-up it's going to be. There are warm-ups throughout which I'm on the verge of quitting. Get out, my head is telling me, skip this workout. There are warm-ups when I can't resist getting on the clock after fifty yards: I start watching the pace clock, pushing for faster times. Four or five hundred yards—five to ten minutes of swimming—ought to be enough. Yet there are times when I'll have some odd little shoulder ache well into the workout proper, and then at 1200 yards it will go away as butter melted in a pan, warmed up at last.

The 200 swim feels fine, and I don't really want to switch to the dull and tedious work of kicking. Resignedly, I grab a kickboard and start. It's bad form to do it with my head up, watching other swimmers, but I do so anyway, chatting with other kickers—as our breathing gets more labored—in adjoining lanes. Eight interminable laps, my legs growing rapidly more leaden with fatigue: boring and painful and boring. Kicking is very slow. It's easier to do yardage when you're moving fast, even if the pace is more exhausting.

That's what makes pulling so much fun: you go fast, you get somewhere. With a float to hold your legs up, you achieve less drag with no effort. Using the smaller arm muscles instead of the big muscles of the legs uses less oxygen, so you don't run out of wind. You feel as if you're never going to get tired. Most swimmers can pull a 500 faster than they will swim a 500 (in workouts, that is—racing is another matter). No matter how I feel otherwise, I always get on the clock for pulling, knowing it's a chance to rack up an interesting time.

The variety of work is to make sure you've used all the major muscle groups. In the warm-up, you want to make sure you've gotten everything just a little bit tired. You want to work all major systems just hard enough so they need a little recovery time. Then you take a break of a minute or so between warm-up and the start of the quality work, and the surge of recovery will send you into your first set on a rising tide. If you don't get everything a little tired during the warm-up, the first wave of fatigue will hit early in the quality work, and it will be discouraging.

In my 200 yards of pulling, I'm surprised to hit the halfway point at 1:15. Not too shabby. I begin to think about trying to finish in 2:30, then remember I'm still supposed to be warming up. I back off, tired enough. I'm ready for a short break.

### 5 × 100 on 1:30

The first set after the warm-up is five 100s in a row, leaving on a new one every minute and a half. My swimming is strong and crisp for the first one, and I finish at 1:08, which is too fast; I'll pay for it very soon. The next one requires a dismaying amount of effort to get below 1:15, which means the rest period shrinks from twenty-two seconds to fifteen seconds just as I'm beginning to get tired. (In this situation seven seconds is a useful rest.) One lap into the third 100, my stroke begins to go ragged, bad habits resurfacing. I try to concentrate on mechanics instead of time; I manage to hold 1:15s but I pay the price, and am very glad that there are only five 100s in the set. I seem to be juggling an awful lot of numbers, but that's part of the way workouts are.

This is distance training, aimed principally at the aerobic system. It's called short-rest interval work. You're trying to train everything to recover as quickly as possible. The changes that training makes in the heart muscle actually occur faster during the first few seconds of recovery time than they do while the overload is going on. Interval training is devised to cash in on this principle.

Short-rest interval work makes you start the next piece of work only partially recovered, which works the long-term delivery capabilities of the aerobic system. For speed training, to improve the anaerobic system, you go to long-rest interval work. You swim each piece nearer maximum speed, and rest much longer—two or three minutes, perhaps—between swims. (See 8 × 50, below.)

Five 100s on 1:30 is a good test but not extreme. In hard training for an important distance race, I will attempt 10 × 100 on 1:20, although I never quite manage to hold that interval through all ten. College swimmers often do 50 × 50 on :50—fifty 50-yard sprints, leaving every fifty seconds. Swimming phenomenon Tracy Caulkins is a legend for doing 100 × 100 on 1:00, or 10,000 yards at a pace that I can't maintain for 200 yards.

### 1 × 500 on 6:30

I spend a couple of minutes getting my breath, swapping jokes with other swimmers, before beginning the 500. Since we're doing only one of them, "on 6:30" just means we're to finish in 6:30 or less. As I swim through the first hundred I struggle through more arithmetic. Six minutes and thirty seconds is 390 seconds, so I've got to average seventy-eight seconds—1:18—for each hundred. This is not going to be easy.

An uninterrupted 500-yard swim requires a slightly different stroke than five 100-yard swims. I concentrate on smoothing everything out, lengthening every move. Since the big leg muscles burn so much oxygen, I try to keep my kick to a minimum, using my legs for not much more than keeping me flat in the water and pointing straight.

I hit the first 100 at 1:15. Out too fast again. Energy requirements go up as a cube of the increase in speed, which means that a 1:15 takes a *lot* more effort than a 1:18. I back off slightly, and, tiring, quickly slip to a 1:20 pace. I try to pick the pace up again but, turning to mush, only hang on. I finish at 6:34, angry with myself for blowing the set. My time ballooned between the 200- and 400-yard marks, which is a bad habit of mine. To maintain an even pace in the face of growing fatigue, you have to push harder on each successive lap. I have trouble making myself remember this in the middle of a hard set.

A single 500 at 6:30 (or 6:34) is also not severe. In serious distance work, 4 × 500 or even 2 × 1650 would not be exceptional. The largest problem with 2000- and 3000-yard sets is maintaining concentration through all those minutes of virtually uninterrupted freestyle. (None of the other strokes is swum at a longer distance than 200 meters.)

We're halfway through the workout.

### 5 × 200 on 3:00, Desc.

This is the toughie: five 200s, leaving every three minutes, descending the times—which means finishing each at a better time than the one that preceded it. I tend to fall into a rut, bringing in each 200 at a rather stately 2:35, which would give me twenty-five seconds' rest between each. Five such 200s is conceivable. The problem is to descend them. The solution is to start out slow, and settle for less rest.

I really dog it through the first, at 2:45. The next comes in at 2:37; I'm no longer loafing, still feeling okay. During the third the fatigue hits hard, and I am in distress, tightening up, feeling the prickly rush at skin surface that means you're pouring sweat underwater. 2:34.

During the fourth 200 I convince myself that I can't continue to descend the times, that I hurt too much to keep this up. I'm out of wind, choking on phlegm, thrashing at the water. I touch the wall at 2:36, three seconds too slow for the descent I am trying to hold. I've been concentrating on hurting, not on swimming. Angry again, I start the last 200 with my jaw set, working hard at holding my technique together. I just try to swim well—and apply a lot of power—and let the pace take care of itself.

It works. I hit halfway at 1:16, and begin telling myself that I can hold *any* pace for another 100 yards. At the start of the last lap I begin a big, full-bore kick that drives me home in 2:30. I've negative-split the last 200, the last half faster than the first, in a kind of doubling of the descending-time effect. Negative splits are admired among swimmers. Despite the poor fourth 200, it's a nice piece of work and I'm proud of it. A small defeat in the 500, a small triumph in the descending 200s. I take a long rest before the next set. Only 600 yards to go.

## *8 × 50 on 2:00*

The last set is speed work. The rationale is that with two full minutes from the start of one 50 to the start of the next— and only little short 50s to swim—you should swim much closer to maximum speed. On the basis of my racing times I should be able to average about thirty seconds for each of the eight 50s. Racing times don't come on the heels of 2000 yards of interval work.

I hate speed training. I'd rather swim slower, with almost no rest between swims, than at close to maximum with several minutes' rest. After four or five 50s I know I will begin to feel vaguely ill, trembling from the exertion, depressed. It is cranking up the will, convincing yourself to go ahead and sprint hard each time—and hold the sprint to the end—that takes it out of you.

We're doing the 50s en masse, six lanes abreast, two swimmers to a lane. Once more the synergy helps: you have someone to race on either side, an aid to focus. We begin. My first 50 is a 31; my second, in disappointment at the first, is a 29; my third, reflecting the effort of the second, a 32. Slowly my times balloon on up to 35 and keep rising. I go slower and slower, a mechanical toy whose batteries are running down. It is a real-life version of the classic nightmare about running in sand. It doesn't hurt that much; my arms just won't work anymore. I give them the same commands that would ordinarily send me sprinting down the pool, but I only cruise. I imagine I can feel the neural signal zing down from my brain to my arm and stop dead, as if hitting a lead shield. Nothing is reaching the place that makes the muscles work.

I've dumped all the energy out of my arm muscles. At the end of an hour's hard work I suspect I don't have much glycogen left. Whatever the biochemistry, I'm out of gas. That's supposed to mean it was a good workout.

### 200 Swim-down

The 200-yard swim-down is R&R, loose, loafing yardage to keep the muscles working gently a little while longer, pumping out the major accumulations of lactic acid and other waste products. The swim-down speeds your immediate recovery—at the end of it you feel you could handle another set—and it markedly reduces tomorrow's fatigue and stiffness. It's tempting to skip it, after 3000 yards, but if I do, I pay for that later, also.

So I goof through the swim-down, trying new wrinkles in my stroke. I begin to feel better. By the time I head for the shower all of the immediate fatigue has been processed away. I have the curious flat, alkaline taste in the back of my throat

that I always get after hard aerobic work. My body temperature is high enough that I can only tolerate a lukewarm shower.

There isn't time for much talk during the workout proper,
so showering and dressing are social occasions. We compare
bitches about the workout, discuss future races, talk sports.
It is a comfortable group. I dress and go to my car still sweat-
ing lightly. Home is twenty-two miles away. On the car radio the Celtics are in the last two minutes against the Bucks,
and losing. After a mile or two of driving through the night I
notice I'm still carrying my shoulders up around my ears. I
take a deep breath and drop them, consciously trying to let go
of the residual tension in all those muscles that have just
worked so hard. A great wave of relaxation begins to sweep
over me. I feel alert, still pumped up, yet extremely peaceful.
And not tired at all: that will hit in another hour or so.

This was a standard workout; there are infinite variations
using different strokes, distances, intervals. (A good coach
keeps mixing things up so the team never recognizes a workout from the past.) There are complex schemes governing the
percentage of the workout time and distance given to each
kind of training, and there are specific drills for aerobic and
anaerobic systems, for attempting to lower the anaerobic
threshold (the switchover point between systems), for developing such things as sprint speed and lactate tolerance.

But in the end every workout is the same: a warm-up,
making sure everything is ready; a series of sets that are varied
in detail but similar in their general effect; a string of recoveries, breathing spells for the organism to refill for the next
effort. All of training, in any sport, is a process of juggling
energy and fatigue, strength and failure.

The fatigue you feel progresses to a point, and then you're
dealing with a fairly steady state. Only in the early stages
does the fatigue come in specific discomforts—pain in the

legs, aching lungs. After awhile that's replaced by a leaden numbness that is not pleasant but also not unbearable. Once you get past the temporary twinges and specific discomforts, fatigue seems more psychological than physical. It manifests itself mostly as a powerful disinclination to continue doing the work.

If specific discomforts continue, you should quit the workout: that's a sign that something is wrong, an injury developing, something not recovered from the last workout. But if what you're feeling is just a growing revulsion at the silly idea of continuing to expend energy, then you have to talk yourself through that. That's just another part of why workouts are the way they are.

You can't do it if it isn't fun. So each set becomes a tactical game, a guerrilla strike into the territory of fatigue, to see how many seconds you can steal and still escape—alive, but well-used—at the end. It is also to see how deeply you can penetrate that territory and survive, but thinking about this during the workout isn't helpful.

# ENGINES

O N E   S A T I S F Y I N G   thing about training—or any other benign obsession—is that it becomes a kind of positive paranoia. You start interpreting all your experience in the light of your new enthusiasm. Everything *applies*: it makes you feel much more connected.

Contemplating the scattered bones on my plate after eating fried chicken, I'm struck by the unfair division of flesh on a bird's body. At my house, as at most other houses, the fleshy breast pieces go first; Aunt Audrey is famous for getting stuck with the bony back pieces. This starts me thinking about the biomechanics of bird flight. The fried chicken shows how it works.

It's the downstroke of the wings that provides the power, the thrust that drives the bird forward and upward into flight. Contraction of the powerful breast and wishbone muscles pulls the wings downward. The upstroke of the wings is only relaxed recovery, pushed by air; no muscle is required. If birds flew upside down part of the time, their bony backs would muscle up—and the back pieces would disappear a lot sooner from the dinner platter. I'll bet the more acrobatic birds—bird-feeder birds, hoverers—have meatier backs than more point-to-point birds like ducks. I'm not going to eat a goldfinch to find out.

Of course, modern chickens don't fly all that much, but the genes are there to lay down muscle against the possibility of a more active life. Chickens mostly walk or stand around, and they have the legs and thighs to show for it. At dinnertime those pieces go next. It's muscle that makes carnivores salivate.

The musculature of birds has other ramifications for athletics. Chicken breasts are composed of white meat—fast-twitch muscle designed for sprinting. Chickens fly, if at all, in short bursts, for which the long, slow delivery of oxygenated energy is not needed. The energy supplies in the muscle itself are sufficient. (Those energy supplies are stored as glycogen, a form of glucose, or sugar. Some say white meat tastes sweeter than dark.) For tasks of longer duration, like standing around, the oxygenated system is more efficient. Endurance muscle—of better oxygenated slow-twitch fibers—is darkened by its more copious blood supply: dark meat. Wild ducks, marathon flyers of the bird world, are mostly dark meat. This is old stuff in exercise physiology, and it's being challenged these days. The evidence, naturally, is that the picture is a lot more complicated than I've sketched it.

I certainly never wanted to become obsessed with muscle. I always used to run with what might be called the antimuscle set. Muscle was a suspicious quantity, a synonym for brute force, the metaphorical opposite of wit. Nothing, I always maintained, was ever solved *that* way. Even when I started into swimming competition, I figured that I was going to outsmart the problem. I would train, sure, but I would go at the whole business so cleverly that I would never need to overpower anything.

It came as no small surprise, then, to discover that it was a growing understanding of muscle—of the stuff itself, the red meat—that has done more than anything else to explain ath-

letics to me. Now, I don't know why that should have surprised me. In school I loved geometry, hated algebra. Muscle
is the most mechanical part of the physiology, working with
concrete, elementary forces and angles. It's the engine of
biomechanics. In the muscle is everything that athletics is
made of.

An errand takes me up a wooded slope behind my house.
As I walk up the steep grade my thighs start to burn. It begins to bother me, but then I get interested: this, too, has to
do with athletics. The discomfort is from muscle fibers that
are running out of energy. I imagine that every time I run
those fibers out of energy, they restore themselves a little
more fully than before. Dumping the fuel out of the muscles
helps accustom them to a generous, even profligate acquisi-
tion and dispensation of the energy stores that make movement possible. I envision the thigh muscles as large sponges,
the energy supplies squeezed out as I walk up the hill, then
sucked back up again from rapidly pumping blood on the
way back down. The oftener that transaction takes place, the
greater their capacity will be. It is an image that keeps my
pace brisk all the way to the top, and I come back down enjoying the surge of recovery that warms my wobbly legs.

I kept at the swimming: intervals, repeat distances, speed
work, over-distance exercises, bulk yardage. Bits and pieces,
small gains accumulated, an occasional setback from a cold or
other interruption. It seldom occurred to me that what I was
training was muscle.

I grew a little. That was haunting at first, my body shift-
ing dimensions, reminding me of adolescence. I had stayed
roughly the same tall (6' 3"), skinny (165–170 lbs.) ecto-
morph through most of the three decades since high school.

With regular training I began to add a thin layer in my upper body while my weight stayed the same. I was used to an added inch now and then at the beltline; around the shoulders, it felt very different. It changed my center of gravity, made me move differently. I enjoyed the continuing reminder of change.

I also began to get stronger, which brought me up short after all those years of brains-versus-brawn foolishness. I had never been particularly strong, and disuse had sapped what basic strength I had. It was the kind of loss that I only noticed when I began getting stronger again. There's little call for force in the way I live, but I noticed the gain just in dealing with my own body weight, in the business of daily life—in getting up and down stairs, in and out of automobiles, in getting myself moving, physically, and getting myself stopped again. I had not been aware that these little pieces of business had begun to wear on me, although I did notice that I'd begun to launch those moves with a more deliberate wind-up. (In *The View from 80*, Malcolm Cowley says one personal signal of aging came when he noticed the pause on the landing before a flight of stairs.)

I only became aware of the way these little energy expenditures were burdening me when, as my muscle tone and general level of strength improved, they lightened. I didn't think I needed to be strong. Then I noticed—when, for example, I spent a day at yard work—that it was useful to be strong all day long. I began to enjoy that, secretly.

Sheepishly, I began fooling around with weights. The rationale was easy enough. I was a middle-aged masters athlete, as interested in gain as anybody else. I had noticed that a lot of young athletes get their skills nailed down first and then, after relying on youth and raw talent for a few years, get serious about getting stronger. I decided I wouldn't mind being a little stronger. I bought a set of weights and started figuring out how to lift them properly. It is an activity that turned out to be completely different from anything I expected, with more complex content than I thought possible in so simple-minded a form of exercise. It started me exploring an entirely new pocket of athletic experience, radically altering the way I thought about swimming and all other physical tasks.

I was shocked at how awkward it was. I felt horribly clumsy, frustrated by the barbell's refusal to do my bidding. I would expect clumsiness at the outset at tennis or golf or any other new sports motion, but this was just picking up a *weight*, right? (This awkwardness must be the mother of the large array of Nautilus, Universal, and other weight machines.) It took me several sessions to figure out that the weights were awkward because I was weak—that, as in any other athletic activity, one had to be able to control the implements, and that the motions would smooth out when I could manage the tools of the trade. Meanwhile, I wobbled.

I'd never before bothered to isolate specific muscles and work them hard. I'd engaged in the usual sports, which work most of the body, but I'd never proceeded methodically from large muscle to large muscle, giving each in turn a good workout. To do so is a revelation. It allows you to focus on a single contraction, to pay attention to precisely how a single muscle or muscle group works. You learn where the strong and weak parts of the range of contraction are, at what angle you use the muscle for maximum effectiveness, what other muscles you bring in when you need more force. You begin to see each muscle or muscle group almost as a separate organ, with its own small environment, its own tools (attachment points, available leverage, range of motion to work with). A weight workout is an anatomy lesson.

I was also surprised to find that I quickly got a rather more complete physical workout with the weights than from a workout at just about anything else. Not a cardiovascular workout, perhaps (although more experienced weight trainers point out that you can do that, too, by proceeding rapidly from exercise to exercise, keeping your heart rate up), but a very thorough soft-tissue workout. A musculoskeletal workout, if you will. Early weight workouts had a way of staying with me, reminding me for twenty-four hours or more that I'd done a heavy load of work. I knew I'd spent an interesting piece of energy.

I began very cautiously, with quite low weights (seldom more than twenty or thirty pounds on the bar) and few repetitions. My muscles got sore anyway. Some say you never stop getting sore from strength-training workouts, at least as long as you're working for rapid gain. I tried to work out every other day or every third day—at any longer interval you don't build strength so much as you just make yourself sore all over again each time. At shorter intervals, the workouts tear down muscle instead of building it up. The system won't stand it.

I discovered some startling weaknesses. I was by this time competing with some success in swimming, and was supposed to be fit. Yet there were exercises designed specifically for swimmers that I couldn't do, not even one repetition, with a four-pound weight in my hand. I was a weight wimp. I may always be.

Weight work, I found, will make you stretch. I have not always been conscientious about stretching exercises. I believe in them, but I don't always practice my philosophy lessons. After, or even *during*, a weight workout, I found myself stopping to stretch. Putting a muscle through enough hard repetitions to bring it to the edge of failure—the textbook description of how to achieve maximum gain—puts it in a state that cries out to be stretched back to resting length again. Weight work reminds me to do my stretching.

Despite some mild soreness, my modest level of strength training left me with an almost immediate sense of gain, just as with any new vigorous activity. Working with weights does pump you up—literally, hydraulically, the muscles engorged with blood. I would feel a bit oversized for several hours afterward. I also struggled with narcissism. I mean I'm not really interested in all that bulging muscle stuff, I swear it, but, geez, would you look at the way that part stands up there, I never knew it did *that*. And I would fall in love with my flexor carpi ulnaris for ten seconds or so, or until the next exercise.

The amusing thing about weight training, though, was that what it really did for me was make me better at handling weight. This isn't as self-evident as it sounds, and, I think, a gain not lightly to be dismissed. Handling heavy objects in the day-to-day business of life—bags of dog food, stove wood, armloads of groceries, books—is not so much a matter of sheer weight-lifting strength as it is of small skills, tricks. To haul the battery out of your car you don't do a military press; you do a series of little cheats and sneaks. Handling heavy things involves angles, balances, leverages. Weight training teaches you those things. It teaches you to take small gains and consolidate them, to get weights into motion and then use the momentum, to put the power into brief bursts to clear thresholds, and to rest in between. That's where the anatomy lesson pays off: it gives you a more solid background in using your own mechanics for solving the problems of human movement.

These are *not* the methods that build strength most quickly; they are just the methods that help you deal with uncomfortable weights. In strength training, the whole point is to take your musculature slowly and evenly through maximum loads. The little tricks of dealing with weights are counter-productive, to be avoided. Tricks are cheating. (Learning to cheat—to handle maximum weights—is the goal of the sport of weight-lifting, a different discipline.) But because you've got an excess of weight to deal with, you have to cheat a bit to manage. That cheating sharpens reactions, sharpens your skill at using your body to generate force, even if it isn't the fastest way to develop muscle fibers. The sharpening of those skills is reassuring. Confronted with a heavy task that used to give me pause, I now just go ahead and do it. Life gets more efficient that way.

There were plenty of times when my training sagged. It wasn't so much that I got bored or tired, but that I would lose my sense of direction. I would continue to do the yardage with no clear idea of what I was trying to accomplish. It took awhile before I learned to have a specific goal, or a specific weakness to work on, in every workout. When all else failed, I found it helpful to think about motor units.

As a boy athlete I could have been had—seduced into greater efforts—if anyone had ever told me about motor units. The muscle fibers that contract to perform any athletic task are grouped into motor units. The signal for contraction reaches the muscle by way of a motor nerve, which branches at the muscle and innervates a multitude of fibers. One motor nerve and all the muscle fibers innervated by it make up a motor unit. When fatigue sets in, the signal still reaches the motor unit, but it finds only fibers that don't have enough energy to contract, or in which lactic acid has temporarily shut down muscle function.

When that happens, you run out of functioning motor units. To keep going you have to recruit new, unfatigued motor units, and these are unaccustomed to performing the task you are now asking them to do. Untrained, unfamiliar motor units aren't likely to allow you to perform the athletic motions as smoothly and surely as you did before you tired. Your form is gone, a victim of fatigue.

Open and close your hand rapidly, keeping it up until fatigue begins to set in. Before long you have to *think* harder—you have to concentrate to keep the motion going. As the muscles of your forearm and hand burn and threaten to cramp, you will begin to vary the rhythm, change the pace, achieve closure only in jerks and spasms. The smooth movement with which you began is gone. You're having to come up with new ways to open and close your hand. You're searching for and recruiting motor units that still have some energy supply.

Recruiting new motor units takes extra effort—more energy is burned by these untrained, less efficient motor units, and more mental effort is needed to find them and put them to use.* So one part of training is to improve the functioning of the familiar motor units, and another is to find as many of the unaccustomed motor units as possible beforehand, and to train them, too, for the task. The more motor units you have available for any task, the better you will be able to perform it. Eight men can move a piano more easily than three men can, if you only keep them coordinated. The more motor units you have available, the more the energy costs can be shared, and thus the longer you can hold off fatigue. Your form, your skill, will last longer.

You try to recruit as many motor units as possible in training in order not to have to venture into the unfamiliar edges of your capacity during competition. The way you train more motor units is to exhaust the motor units you ordinarily use

---

*Mental effort requires an expenditure of energy that is approximately the same, chemically, as that required to fire muscle cells. I have trouble remembering this, perhaps because my brain cells are tired.

for a task, and then to keep on performing the task, or attempting to perform the task. It is not particularly pleasant to work your trained motor units to exhaustion in the first place, and it also is not pleasant to attempt to continue with a combination of exhausted but well-trained motor units and fresh but completely untrained motor units. Fatigue makes the discomfort that tells you the training is having an effect. Knowing this doesn't actually reduce that discomfort, but it allows you to separate it from the kind of sensations that they give novocaine for.

We don't know how muscle works. I was talking to Tom McMahon, the scientist who, with Peter Greene, designed Harvard University's tuned indoor track. I asked him about scientific frontiers remaining in his field of biomechanics. "There are still plenty of great mysteries left in muscle research," he told me. "If you wanted me to look straight up and say what is the most exciting work being done in science, I believe it is the work going on at the level of interaction of actin and myosin at the cross bridge."

Actin and myosin are the rack and pinion of the muscle fiber. If you look closely enough into the muscle cell—with an electron microscope—you finally reduce things to two kinds of strands of protein, actin and myosin. Bunches of these strands lie parallel, and slide over each other telescopically when the muscle contracts. (Put the fingertips of one hand against those of the other hand, then slip the fingers together. That, mechanically, is how muscle contracts.) Contraction is caused by an electrochemical transaction, the formation of cross bridges between the two kinds of fibers, and a kind of molecular ratcheting action that causes the strands to crawl along each other's length.

We think. This is the freshman physiology view of muscle contraction. Start by asking how the muscle contracts; at each new mechanical step (multiplying the magnification of the electron microscope), ask again, *Why?* The textbooks keep giving answers until you get to the cross bridges and the electrochemical transaction. If you keep asking why, the texts stop giving facts and start speculating. You are into an area where modern physiology is still at work.

"Understanding what causes the force in the muscle," McMahon said, "and the process by which chemical energy gets converted over into mechanical energy plus heat, that's a tantalizing question. How the muscle works is a question that has the same dignity and importance as the questions the nuclear scientists were asking in the twenties and thirties. They were asking, What is the atom like? How is it organized? What happens when you disturb it? Once you know the answers to those questions, you know everything about chemistry, everything about matter.

"In biology," McMahon went on, "the question about muscle is supremely important in the organization of living things. It's really only muscle that separates living animals from dead ones. We are only alive because our hearts pump blood and our diaphragms pump air and we have the ability to move. That's all muscle. Maybe you prefer to say we're alive because our brain works, but I really think the brain was designed to coordinate the activities of the muscle. We don't know how the muscle works. We can say we think these are the steps along the way, but that's still just begging the question."

# EIGHT
# CLOSURE

A T   T H E   B E G I N N I N G of my training I thought my biggest job would be psychological: to learn to continue making effort when I didn't feel much like doing so. Now the task seems almost purely muscular. Training is processing energy, and energy has become a more tangible quality. It has recently been faddish to talk about energy as a kind of nervous power, a glittery excitement, mystical. It is no such thing. Energy is that stuff you can dump right out of the muscles, which then comes pouring back in again.

I am beginning to understand muscular contraction, but the picture is hazy. How does this really work? I place my hand flat on the desk, letting it lie there of its own weight. I begin to press down, and then gradually increase the force, bringing in more motor units. The muscle of my triceps begins to stiffen. Contraction seems to start in the center of the cross section of the muscle and spread outward to the periphery, and to start in the middle of the length of the muscle and spread toward the elbow and the shoulder. As it spreads I feel the locked-up stiffness that signals a muscle at work. As I increase the downward force on my hand, the stiffening turns the corner at the elbow and starts involving forearm muscles, the wrist. At the same time my shoulder muscles and the tendons that delineate the armpit tighten to provide a brace. I use that brace to reach across my upper body, in search of more motor units, even beginning to use muscles of my breast and back to increase the force, finding a way to put part of my body weight onto the downward-pressing hand. I am reminded of some cartoon creature, the stiffness of contraction spreading gradually across my entire body.

If I apply enough pressure, the joints of wrist, elbow, and shoulder begin to complain, asked to withstand pressure without the lubricating effect of motion. Joints don't like that. Apply *enough* pressure and fatigue sets in, and, yes, it begins to hurt. This entire process is turned on and off, in dozens of different muscles, in every swimming stroke.

When you really work the muscle, but before you can quite call the sensation pain, it starts "singing" to you. The song is body-builders' theme music, the anthem of muscle growth; you work the muscle until you get "a hard burn," the vibratory ache of fatigue. The muscle's response to that burn, over time, is to add cross section. Hypertrophy, the phenomenon that makes the muscle grow bigger, is another mystery. Athletes have always known that if you work a muscle regularly it gets larger. Physiologists have confirmed this with countless experiments, but so far can't say how the muscle grows, or why it happens.

I've heard one scientist speculate, not for attribution, that it might be histamine (a colorless fluid released when cells are injured) that stimulates muscle fiber to new growth. Electron microphotography reveals disklike bands across the fibers, called "Z-bands." In some cases, ruptures across the faces of these bands would seem to lead to a method of repair that would lay down new muscle. The technology, the scientific cleverness to check it out, isn't there yet. Working the muscle to the point of fatigue, even of damage, seems to be involved. Some trainers say that if you don't work the muscle hard enough to make it at least slightly sore, you haven't accomplished anything. No pain, no gain. But we don't know what causes muscle soreness either, really. It is assumed to be the result of microscopic tears in the muscle tissue, combined with the resulting edema and accumulation of wastes, but we're not sure.

Muscles are encased in sacs of connective tissue. The connective tissue thickens at each end of the muscle and turns into tendon, which attaches the muscle to bone. A lot of interesting action in the muscle is in the vicinity of the conversion to tendon. There is some evidence that eccentric contractions—the contractions you use to resist lengthening of the muscle, as when you lower a heavy weight—stimulate muscle growth more than ordinary lifting, concentric contractions do.

Eccentric contractions make you sorer than the other kind. Walking downhill, which requires eccentric contractions of the leg muscles, makes you sorer than walking uphill. Some physiologists believe that it is the harsh stretching out of the muscle-to-tendon conversion area that makes maximum soreness, when a stretching force works against a contracting force. The other kind of stretching—programmatic stretching of relaxed muscles as a warm-up and warm-down procedure—has been shown to help prevent soreness in the first place, and to help sore muscles recover after the damage has been done.

At the height of my weight training, when I was also swimming a couple of thousand yards a day, circumstances caused me to walk for about three hours on city sidewalks. Twenty-four hours later my calves were so sore I was limping.

I was shocked. I had been doing a weight exercise specifically aimed at conditioning and strengthening those calf muscles. When I was in such good shape, how could my muscles betray me so?

I should not have been surprised. I was overlooking the elusive quality of specificity. No exercise can exactly duplicate any other. The only real way to condition the muscles you use in fast walking is by walking fast.

An exercise physiologist told me of an experiment in which a four-minute miler was put on a treadmill churning away at a four-minute-mile pace. All the runner had to do was keep up the pace for four minutes. He couldn't do it. "He couldn't get enough *rest*," the physiologist told me. He couldn't vary the pace, let motor units A and B recover while motor units X and Y took over. He was denied the luxury of backing off or pressing ahead. Every quarter mile had to be clocked off in exactly sixty seconds. The runner had learned, at considerable cost, how to run a four-minute mile; on the treadmill there wasn't enough time, enough flexibility, for him to use that knowledge. The machine-made regularity of the pace ground him down.

The romantic part of me says that for truly superior performance, you have to introduce the opportunity for creativity into the equation. You have to take into account human variability. The more rational part of me says that treadmill was just too damned specific.*

When I first got started training, it didn't seem right that any unaccustomed activity would make me stiff and sore for a couple of days. I hated to back off while I was still enjoying new activities, just because I knew if I continued I'd be sore

---

*Since I heard this story some Englishmen have held treadmill championships. The winner ran 3:59 flat. His fastest time on an outdoor track had been 3:59.8, so my point about specificity is somewhat diluted.

later. I had this fantasy that if I got back into shape I might avoid the inevitable revenge of the muscles.

I was wrong, of course; it doesn't get any better. Soreness is the downside of muscularity, the other side of the coin of enjoyable movement. It is somehow tied to the fact that muscle is a one-way medium, which can do one thing and one thing only: contract. There is no physiological mechanism to de-contract the muscle. We can relax the muscle—usually—but that's all.

There are some automatic relaxing mechanisms. Kick with your leg and you contract the quadriceps; at the same time a signal is sent to the antagonist muscles in the hamstring to relax them. Some athletic trainers feel that muscle pulls can result from failure of this system. They say you don't often pull the muscle you're working hardest, you pull its opposite number. Maybe it's neurological noise, interfering with the signal for relaxation. In your effort to recruit more motor units you recruit the wrong ones; they pull the wrong muscles tight, and pop goes the hamstring. I haven't been able to confirm this notion in the literature.

Merely relaxing the muscle doesn't quite restore it to its uncontracted state. To do that—to finish the process that contraction began—you have to pull it back out to length. Nowadays everyone advises stretching exercises as a warm-up before hard exercise and as a cool-down afterward. You manipulate your skeleton to take each limb through its range of motion, making sure every possible muscle is pulled out to length. Nobody pretends that stretching is going to pull every single strand of actin back down along the length of its myosin neighbor, until all are precisely at the maximum resting length again, but it does help to pull things—gently, gradually—in that direction.

We do a lot of stretching, willy-nilly, whether or not we exercise or lift weights. When we arise from our desks after a long stint of intense work, when we get up from our theater seats, when we get out of bed in the morning—after any extended period of immobility—we will stretch. We do it for pleasure. We tend to lose sight of that. All of this athletic stretching is only an extension of that natural human urge, done a little more systematically, a little more consciously. Once you become conscious of how good it feels, it isn't that hard to make it a regular part of your routine—particularly when it helps make soreness go away.

I stopped getting sore from ordinary, daily training quickly enough, adapting to that specific set of uses. I also rarely suffered any of the various pulls and tears and charley horses from injury, the ones that come from *really* overdoing it. Swimming is relatively innocuous in that sense. But there is a third kind of muscle pain, less easy to understand, that plagues me yet. Sometimes for no discernible reason I am left with knots, spasms, hot spots, with strips of muscle so charged—so wanting discharge—that they almost give off sparks. I get the image of Leyden jars full of static electricity.

Muscle as electrical condenser: it's a useful conceit. As I write this I am trying to relax the ridge of tension between my shoulder blades, but of course I can't. It only feels like a hot soldering iron has been inserted under the skin of my back; it's just muscle tissue, uselessly contracted. It's as if it was left contracted, overlooked, while my conscious control of such matters went on to attend to other things. It happened so long ago that now I can no longer find the entry point, the way to reach in there and flip the switch to turn things off. *Usually* we can relax the muscle. But it gets away from us, tightening in spasms of fatigue, surrounding itself with neurological numbness that voids our control.

After a long, hard workout, my back may feel like a sack full of hot doorknobs. That can be worked out. After a long, hard day of nonworkouts—business meetings, airplanes and taxis, family discussions—it is much worse. Using the muscles is a lot easier on them, whatever the level of fatigue that results, than holding them ready for use but never firing them off in movement. This, too, must be part of the fight-or-flight syndrome. I'd thought of that only as a hormonal effect, from the lack of opportunity for the system to process and get rid of the adrenaline and other emotionally triggered products of stress. But the effects of thwarted action seem to reach far beyond hormonal overkill. Those effects must filter right on down to the level of interaction of actin and myosin at the cross bridges.

When a muscle is held in contraction, either deliberately or from spasm, energy is burned. It gets tired. Fatigue produces waste materials. Without movement—without the pumping action of muscular contraction and relaxation—circulation is impaired. The wastes can't be fully flushed out of the tissues. The fatigue can't be relieved, even with the "rest" of inactivity. That's the reason that any hard exercise should be followed by a cooling down, gradually tapering off with gentle movement.

It could well be that every knot, every spasm, has as its seed some minuscule muscle tear or other injury. The muscle's reaction to pain is to contract. Whatever the initial cause, the system reads the pain and the buildup of wastes as an injury. It reacts by immobilizing the area to prevent additional injury from movement of the affected parts. It does it hydraulically, packing the area with bags of fluid (swollen cells) until it is, in effect, splinted. Restricted movement of the area leads to further stagnation, further buildup of waste products, further isolation of the muscle from the relief it requires. The hard, swollen knot (you can feel it with your fingertips) is inflamed with pain for a while. Eventually it goes almost numb, accessible only to heavy pressure. People who rarely get their backs rubbed are often shocked at how much hidden pain they are carrying around back there.

Pick the metaphor that works for you: I understand the knots in my back most clearly by the image of the Leyden jar. Pain, as a neurological signal, is an electrical charge. There's a lot of other electricity in the muscle. The signal that starts the contraction is electrical. The energy for the contraction itself comes from the swapping of free radicals—positive electrons flipped loose from one biochemical compound to bind onto the negative electrons in another biochemical compound. The linkages at the cross bridges are also formed by electrochemical bonds between positively and negatively charged atoms (we think). Electromyography is the technique for measuring this electrical component of muscular activity; contract a muscle and the electromyographic strip chart becomes an incoherent mass of squiggles from the bursts of electricity. I don't know if the same electrical noise is associated with muscles in spasm, but my back, as full of static as an old radio, tells me it should be.

Sarah, aged two, demonstrates another version of this matter of unresolved energy. Offered her choice from a tray of candies, she ponders thoughtfully until excitement overcomes her. The tension of the decision finally starts her bobbing up onto her toes, then literally jumping in place. She calms herself and considers some more, then begins to bounce again. She raises her arms above her head and shakes her hands, as if trying to fling off unusable neural signals—the signals that tell her just to go ahead and *grab*. She, too, is filled with unresolved electricity, generated by emotion, but she is still true enough an animal to discharge the excess. She jumps, she shakes her hands, as if to burn up the energy before it paralyzes her.

I think of the chains they used to hang behind big trucks,

that dragged on the pavement to drain off static electricity. It's as if Sarah jumps and shakes her hands to avoid burning out her voltage regulator. I keep getting this image of a hallway outside the boardroom, and a group of dignified men in three-piece suits, jumping up and down and shaking their hands over their heads before the big merger.

The trouble with muscle is that there's no closure to it. We want some sense of completion, some signal that says that we are fully contracted or fully relaxed, that we've done something besides slide along a continuum and then run out of room to move. We want some signal that correlates with the on-or-off nature of the signal that fires the muscle. We measure off work with numbers—laps completed, weights lifted, seconds chopped off—to give us some mental purchase, since the muscles give us no such signals.

A lot of athletes fall in love with chiropractic. It must be all the snapping and popping. When a chiropractor cracks your back, you get the feeling of something changed, fixed—in chiropractic terms, adjusted. The minuscule realignment of bone ends is usually accompanied by the firing off of some crackingly fine nerve impulses, reinforcing the idea of a moment before which things are wrong, and after which things are right. It's all fixed now. It's very satisfying.

I think we ought to get some kind of signal like that from the muscles. They ought to be fitted with pawls, things that click into place, counting off the length of the contraction. Come to think of it, they are, down there at the level of the cross bridges. We just aren't tuned fine enough to pick it up. Unless that's the singing that they do for us when we use them hard.

There's a 15-year-old cat at our house who has lived a normal long full life, and now mostly dozes through her days in a good-natured feline haze. She's healthy, but she doesn't *weigh* anything anymore. Picking her up is like plucking the puffball from a dandelion stem. She's lost most of her lean muscle mass. She was extremely quick and playful years ago, but she doesn't move around much anymore. She's quit working for a living.

Maybe the exercise physiologists could use lean muscle mass as a kind of activity index. (Twenty-two percent body fat? It's not what you're eating, it's that you're not moving enough, sir.) There is no muscle that is unearned, and it is earned in the most purely lunch-bucket, work-ethic sense of earning. That seems fair. What seems not so fair is that you even have to work to keep it.

# DOING
# PHYSIOLOGY

MY SCHEDULE IS arranged for heavy training now, carrying maximum work loads, trying to tweak the rate of increase. I've just done my second workout of the day. This is not without its costs, leaving me slumped in front of the TV, watching some late-night documentary on penguins, waiting for my metabolism to pipe down so I can sleep. Finally I groan my way to my feet and flip off the set. I take the first few steps toward the bedroom with my knees slightly bent, increasing the load on my quadriceps, checking out the soreness in my thighs. This is a tiring way to walk even when you aren't sore. It's more efficient to stand upright and use bone rather than muscle to support your weight.

As I undress I smile at my brief duck walk, feeling—literally—childish. Kids are always experimenting with other ways of walking, trying this goofy gait or that in the immature little R&D facilities of their bodies. They're finding out what tires them and what doesn't: fatigue will trim the flash off any movement.

My soreness is a product of too much weight work. A siege of flu wiped out a week of swimming workouts, and I tried to make up the difference with more weight training. My assumption is that I've developed strength, but the new muscle

hasn't yet been recruited into swimming motor units. Watch
out for this kind of "intuitive physiology," warns an exercise
physiologist friend. It's usually wrong.

When you train hard and maintain a stiff competition
schedule, athletic considerations do try to sweep everything
else out of your mind. Movement, effort, and energy are the
raw materials from which you are trying to fashion a higher
level of physical efficiency, and you begin to see everything in
those terms. They tend to give you an accelerating sense of
physical possibility, which is a fairly effective antidote for the
more depressing effects of aging. But they also take over your
mind. The metaphors by which I now understand things
have to do with power generated by biochemical transactions, with distribution of fuels, with the laying down of specific strengths against future needs. I find myself trying to
puzzle out the physiology of flight as I watch goldfinches
flutter around the bird feeder. Through processes that I can
trace in myself, from training, I begin to understand more
clearly how Chris's tomato plants grow.

So I am always doing physiology in my head. As I train, or
race, or come across something interesting in my own subjective experience, I find myself stopping to ask, Okay, what's
the physiology for this? Why does this happen? Usually I
have to figure out the physics before I can figure out the
physiology.

Attempting to get my yardage back on schedule, I've dou-
bled up swimming workouts, doing 7000 yards, or about
four miles, in one day. The energy conversion charts say this
is roughly equivalent to sixteen miles of running. This is not
an unheard-of amount of yardage—much less than any serious college swimmer's daily grind—but it's a lot for me, and
I feel it. Runners regularly do this kind of mileage, knocking
it off without much fuss. They tell you to throw in a twelve-
to twenty-mile day now and then, particularly if you're train-

ing for a marathon. They don't tell you how you will feel after that kind of work load.

After any late evening workout I have trouble getting to sleep. My body heat is elevated, my heart rate up. A large bowl of ice cream helps, but it is slow to take effect. (I rationalize the ice cream as one of the fringe benefits of a 4500-calorie day.) If the evening workout has been the second session of the day, I am still wired but also bushed. The metabolic rate is more willing to settle down when the muscles from head to foot are humming in protest, making me feel as if I've been left on the burner at a low simmer. It's a delicious fatigue. Gradually I relax—stretching helps—and begin to sink toward sleep, the bitching of the musculature cooling out, to be replaced by the floating luxury of recovery. I love this state.

On my way downward toward unconsciousness, I ponder the day's effort. The workouts were in different pools, in the morning at the slow Y, at night at the fast junior high school. Some swimming pools just let you go faster. There are several tricks in pool design to increase speed, mostly having to do with control of the water's turbulence. The Y pool has none of them. I get much better workouts at the junior high, which is always a dependable delight.

I'd always assumed that the slowness of the slow pool was a result of choppy waves that kept me bobbing around, up and down, unable to maintain a straight line. Lost motion—travel in unproductive directions—seemed the most likely explanation for the slow times and high levels of effort. But, thinking of the slow pool as I sink toward sleep, I get the image of a handful of cottonseed hulls. I realize that the biggest difference between the pools is the very quality of the water in my hands as I swim. I can't quite get hold of the water in the slow pool; it is turbulent in a way I hadn't thought of before. The swirling, eddying mess in the slow

pool is too busy. I just can't get a decent grip on it. (A pool
with too many people in it is unpleasant to swim in because of
the busy water. At large swimming meets everyone warms up
at the same time, and you'll have six or eight swimmers per
lane. I finally learned to get in early, while I can still get a
sense of what the pool is like in racing condition—i. e., still.)

The curious difference between recreational swimming
and competitive swimming is that when you swim for fun,
much of your pleasure comes from the fluidity of the medium
in which you swim. In competition swimming, you're trying
to turn that fluid into a solid. You're trying to move fast
enough, generate enough force, to overcome the fluidity of
the water, to turn it into a kind of jellied solid that will allow
you to get firm hand and foot plants in it, in order to yank
yourself down the pool. In dreams I often swim as if pulling
myself along a rope slung beneath the surface of the water.
You don't really swim that way—swimming stroke mechanics are much more complicated than that—but the image is
useful. If you can't get a grip on the rope, your hands slip and
waste effort. It is frustrating. My fast pool is deep, calm,
cool, above all dense—a dark blue race course that always rewards effort with fast times. Going back to the slow pool feels
like punishment.

In *The Shell Game*, Olympic rower Stephen Kiesling describes "seat-racing" for the last remaining berth on the U.S.
team for the 1979 World Championships. He is locked into a
tense duel with a Harvard rower named Gardiner. The two
candidates swap back and forth in four-man boats, attempting to demonstrate a clear ability to make a boat go faster
irrespective of the composition of the remainder of the crew.

As the session begins, Steve discovers that Gardiner has
chosen "Marcella," a particular oar that Steve had grown to
prefer in earlier workouts. "Using any of the other oars, I had

tended to 'wash out,' but Marcella was pitched differently and seemed to compensate for whatever it was I had been do-ing wrong." There is much nervous jockeying with the unfa-miliar new oar—"In the warm-up I could barely keep the oar buried in the water through the stroke"—but with the help of some layers of electrical tape in the oarlock, Steve over-comes the handicap and wins the seat.

By happy chance I got to know Steve later and asked him about oars. The physics—and the biomechanics—of it fasci-nated me. The pitch of the oar is governed by the relationship of the angle of the blade to the thole pin, which is the axis around which the oar rotates. The pin's angle is adjustable by loosening a nut. "This adjustment is most easily done on shore but can be done by the coach from the bow of his launch," Steve told me in a letter. "Generally, if the adjust-ment is tried on the water, the nuts fall in the river. So too does the coach. That happened once to my knowledge."

What fascinates me is how critical to the athletic task of rowing is the angle of the thole pin. If the pin is cocked too far in one direction, the blade of the oar will try to leap out of the water when you pull on it. If it is cocked in the other direc-tion, the blade will try to dive. In the first case, you have to use muscular effort to hold the blade in the water; in the sec-ond case you work to keep it from diving too deep. In either case you lose the more efficient straight-line pull of a properly aligned oar, and burn off energy pulling through an ellipse. Rowing is one of the most grueling energy-burns in all of sports anyway, and to squander some of that energy strug-gling with a balky oar is surely madness. It is just this kind of wasted energy from a minor misalignment that makes ath-letes so attentive to detail. It teaches them physics.

Until I saw the documentary on penguin life I never dreamed how well those buffoon birds move in the water:

penguins swim better than some birds fly. There are other athletic pointers to be absorbed from penguin life. The parent birds tease their chicks with food, holding it just out of reach, which makes the young birds exercise, stretching their muscles—progressively overloading their systems—in order to grow stronger. The training effect, applied by penguin mommies.

I also notice that neither the penguins nor the sea lions that prey on them use very large motions to move so fast through the water. They save their large motions—extremely clumsy ones—for attempting to deal with dry land. Then I think of the other aquatic creatures, and realize that none of them uses large motions to swim. The real swimmers are superbly subtle in their efforts. Only man thrashes and flounders, swinging limbs in 360-degree circles, kicking out wildly at improbable angles. We're not very good swimmers. We don't have this activity down yet. The observation starts me thinking about efficiency.

Years ago I thought I might race automobiles. A series of short, sharp lessons convinced me that this wasn't a good idea, but I still found the sport interesting. I hung around motor racing as a journalist for several years.

From time to time I would watch a new young driver come along, another in the succession of rookie sensations. The newcomer would characteristically show great flair and a clear ability to handle a racing car at the limits, to take large risks and get away with them. He would be blazingly fast. He would usually not demonstrate a consistent ability to win big races. As his machines got more powerful, as he competed at higher levels, he would begin, now and then, to crash. If he survived this period and matured as a racing driver, it was always because he—or she—finally learned the most difficult lesson in driving: smoother is faster. Always. Instructors at racing driving schools say their most difficult task is to get the students to slow down and get smooth first, before trying to learn to go *really* fast. Given enough horsepower, almost anyone can go fast—for a while.

I left motor racing behind and began to write about ski racing. I kept quizzing the coaches, trying to learn what makes a good ski racer. The most consistent answer: he—or she—"rides a flat ski." Look at the rooster tails thrown up by the skis, the experts told me. A large spray of snow indicates too much ski edge against the snow, and thus friction, drag. The skier is scrubbing off speed, just like a racing car with its tail hung out. The good racer gets off his edges earlier in the turn than his rivals. He is *"on* his skis," in such a state of balance and control that he can get on and off his edges delicately. He gets smooth.

Chris enjoys professional basketball but resisted the college game. Finally she watched one. "They *jump* in such crazy ways," she said, and captured perfectly the hyperactive quality of the college game. That's exactly it: they move too much. Every gesture carries too far, is yanked back and countermanded the instant it is initiated. The same contrast strikes me when I flip the dial from a pro football game to a college game. The pros appear smooth to the point of lethargy beside the college players' jittery excitability. Usually the "lazy" pro is more effective at his task than the quivering college athlete. When a college athlete turns pro, the most difficult adjustment to the professional game must be to damp down excess motion, to focus and cool-out and smooth over. To learn that smoother is faster.

All of that excess motion—the racing car with its tail hung out, the ski that throws up a great rooster tail, overthrowing, over-jumping, running past the play—wastes the very stuff that the athlete has expended so much effort to produce or acquire. Once you've got the horsepower, you get faster by attention to detail, by learning to keep everything pointed straight ahead, by pulling in a straight line, by getting the power to the ground. How can I apply this in swimming?

"What Nolan Ryan has to do," says Don Drysdale at the beginning of the baseball broadcast, "is check his mechanics at the start, not try to over-throw, and stay within himself." Or as they told you in junior high school, stop trying too hard. To play within yourself means to perform at a level of effort that is within your training experience. To try too hard is to try to recruit untrained motor units. To do so may confuse your carefully practiced motion with extraneous signals. It will take you beyond your comfortable reach, outside your center of gravity, into areas of movement that require unusual feats of balance and recovery—which burn up excessive energy.

Trying harder is not necessarily the way to set new records. It is more likely the way to lose your timing. To do your athletic job not only do you have to get the bat, the glove, the ski edge to the right location at the right time, but you have to get it there in sufficient control to use it properly. If to get there you have pushed too hard, reached too far, you have very likely invested too much time in one segment of the motion at the expense of the next segment, which means that the internal rhythm of the motion is distorted. Violating your carefully learned and manageable time frame for the motion is tantamount to abandoning your skill. Attempting to get the timing back by forcing the issue not only screws up the skill and wears you out, but also invites injury.

Building endurance, then, seems to require the specific training of motor units. Building strength also depends on motor units. Maintaining form seems to require some work with motor units. Then there's skill, which turns out to depend a lot on motor units, too. Just when I think I've got athletics all broken down into nice, discrete, understandable categories, the physiology comes along and ties it back together in tangled loops.

Jim Johnsen and I had just swum a 500-yard freestyle race and were discussing it afterward. Jim is two years younger than I, manager of a ship's bridge simulator for training supertanker captains for Grumman on Long Island. One of us had just beaten the other by a few seconds. I honestly don't recall who won this one. We tend to alternate wins, at a given meet one of us sharper in the short events, the other in the long ones, depending on how training has gone in preceding weeks. Jim also wins races in the other strokes, while I swim only freestyle.

"You really have to keep pressure on your hands, don't you?" Jim said. I didn't know what he meant at first; then I understood. You have to press all the way in a long race. One way you do that is literally by keeping pressure on your hands. I'd thought of the same thing but upside down: if I started to get really tired, I noticed, I would often ease off by letting my wrists go a little slack, so I didn't get quite as firm a pull. Therefore it took less muscle—fewer motor units—to pull through the stroke. I took the pressure off my hands. I also lost speed. But in the rigorous linearity of these processes, reduction of the muscular effort almost immediately reduces oxygen requirements. By reducing pressure on my hands, I got my breath back. This makes it an awful temptation, along about 400 yards into a race, to ease up the pressure on my hands.

To keep pressure on your hands, you have to concentrate on keeping your hand and wrist precisely angled for maximum pull. You keep them precisely angled by firing motor units. To find and recruit more motor units—to make sure you're finding and recruiting the right motor units—you have to do your training with your hands and wrists precisely angled. Concentrate. To keep opening and closing your hand when it begins to get very tired—to dig down and find extra, fresh motor units—you have to concentrate on finding new ways to open and close the hand. To play within yourself, avoiding the use of untrained motor units, you have to concentrate on duplicating the levels of effort at which you trained. To continue any sports motion after the trained motor units are exhausted, you have to concentrate on maintaining your most efficient form, to make the most of the dwindling motor units you have left. To get a strong enough neural signal to the motor unit to activate unfamiliar, untrained muscle fibers, you have to concentrate like the very dickens. You even have to concentrate to maintain your pace while striding up a steep hill. I'm not sure how you do this. There is a mental state required—in training, in performance—that I'm not too familiar with. I have something else to learn. I had no idea that this, too, was part of being an athlete.

# KINESTHETIC
# JUNKIE

S O  T H E R E  I  A M  swimming along, grinding out the yardage, minding my own business, when—after a year of fairly heavy training—my swimming stroke suddenly unfolds for me, like one of those Japanese paper flowers that open up underwater. I stop in the middle of a set—breaking the unwritten law of workouts—to hang on the gutter and think about it for a moment. It is almost eerie in the clarity with which it happens.

I suspect I began concentrating on one small part of the stroke and gained a bit more control of that, which gave me a better feel for the next part, and so on. I don't know how it happened, but what had been one sweeping continuous motion just broke open for me, becoming a linked series of discrete moments. Oh, I thought, so *that's* what I've been doing. Suddenly I had room in which to make small adjustments—an inch or two here, a fraction of a second there, to change what I was doing. I had a much firmer sense of the angles and relationships and relative loadings of the anatomy I was using. I could begin to hunt for more effective purchase. I could in effect invent a whole new stroke every time I put my hand into the water, trying something else in search of gain.

The hard part is trying to figure out how to take advantage of this new perception. There are too many variables. You can't measure the result of any single stroke, you can only time fairly large segments of the distance covered. There's too much to keep up with. But there is all this variation, this room and time in which to experiment. It makes you think that anything is possible.

During high school summers I worked as a lifeguard and swam a great deal. There would come a period near the end of the season when I noticed a change in my swimming. I seemed to get much stronger: every stroke would drive me through the water faster than I expected. (I would first notice the change by the sound of the water rushing past my ears.) It wasn't just in hard swimming but in everything I did in the water. All the minor transactions between poolside, ladder, diving board became almost effortless.

It always seemed to happen just days before the pool closed. The angle of light would change, the Texas sun would stop being quite so brutal, the mornings would be almost too cool for swimming, and I would suddenly find myself with this new power in the water. It drove me nuts: here I was in such positive control, able to get so much more out of every movement, and they were about to close the pool for the winter. Next summer I would have to start all over again at the beginning.

That was kinesthetic sense, I think. Over the summer I would eventually put in enough swimming time to acquire a more accurate reading of what was going on between the water and my flesh, and act more positively on that reading. I wasn't really that much stronger, I was just more effective.

Sports require the translation of desire into motion. You want to get into this or that position, to be over there, to get there faster. You ask your physiology to perform the task.

The better you can read your own state (body position, force loadings, energy level), the better you can carry out the task. Kinesthetic sense is the capacity to read all that, and to respond with the most effective motions. That's what had the water rushing past my ears in the last days of my adolescent summers. It is also what made my stroke open up for me, thirty summers later, and begin taunting me to improve it.

This kinesthetic sense is what teaches the skier to ride a flat ski, the racing driver to learn that smoother is, finally, faster. It is the capacity to sense the forces that will be needed and to marshal them; to perceive the forces at work and to cut through them in the quickest, cleanest way. As with the Taoist cook, asked why his knife never needs sharpening: simple, he says, he doesn't cut the meat, he just uses his knife to separate it, following the natural divisions of the flesh.

I never learned to ski well enough. I was a slow learner, never quite making the transition to a high level of skill. I knew what was involved. I studied the sport, understood the fine points, even wrote a successful book about ski technique. But I never acquired the kinesthetic sense to ski as well as I thought I should. This, too, drove me crazy. I watched the instructors, the racers, who work the snow the way hawks work the wind, and I could almost feel what information they were acting upon. I never quite learned to act upon it. My muscles never caught up with my ideas.

We forget that muscle is as much sensor as it is power source. Half of the neural supply of the muscles is dedicated not to firing off contractions but to gathering information. When we speak of muscle we usually mean the stuff we act with, muscle as effector. But half the muscle's neural capacity is devoted to finding out what the effector part needs to be more effective.

Muscle isn't really involved in the traditional five senses, but those senses constitute only our first line of preparation for the world. Beyond the first five are all the rest of the neurological information-gatherers that locate, arrange, balance, prepare us for response. They are the various mechanoreceptors, located throughout the body, that are fired by movement and weight and change of direction. They read and report on—and improve the capacity for response to—all of the action in which our musculoskeletal systems take part.

We don't think of muscle as a sensor because we know sensory information comes from nerve endings, not flesh. These receptors are in fact nerve endings, buried within the muscles, and the anatomy texts treat them as part of our neural, rather than our muscular, equipment. But they are fired by the muscle that surrounds them. The stimulus that fires the nerve originates in the muscle. Different forms of nerve endings are capable of taking different kinds of readings, making the proprioceptors into a neurological armamentarium organized around action. Maybe muscle isn't such one-way stuff after all. Here's the other part—the part that makes muscle smart.

It's the part that is responsible for the quality of our physical response to the world. Every aspect of athleticism (I still hate that word), from the subtleties of good hands to the explosive thrust of all-out muscular effort, is characterized first by its quick responsiveness, its liveliness. The sensor part of the muscle's neural supply is what turns that liveliness on. Muscle is a suit of power, but it is also a suit of sensitivity, of response. Training gives that part of the physiology a workout too. It is amenable to training. Use makes it work better.

After swimming hard through a two-day meet—improving or equalling my previous best times in five individual events and swimming a couple of relay legs—I sit at the table practically twitching from fatigue, trying to keep my face out of my dinner plate. I drift off into a three-minute trance over the differences between hot and cold foods, what temperature does for flavor, how heat hides fat content. Profound stuff like that, which I somehow had not thought about before. I am conscious of the texture of the tablecloth, of the sounds of silverware on china. I am falling asleep in my chair, but on the way to unconsciousness all of my sensors are pumping away at concert-hall levels. I am flooded with small, intense pleasures. Bring on some Tabasco sauce; let's have some more *sensation* here.

It's as if my five senses are rubbed raw. If that's so, imagine the state of all those other receptors, the ones that work together to give me kinesthetic sense. In the later events of the meet I was tiring, flailing the water, feeling increasingly ineffectual as a swimmer—but my times were holding up, even improving. Despite my leaden arms, I must have been swimming relatively well. To do that I had to substitute efficiency and control for fading power. I must have been getting good information from those kinesthetic receptors. The racing weekend must have given that part of me a terrific workout.

Then it strikes me, jerking my head up out of my mashed potatoes with the suddenness of the thought: maybe *that's* how training increases skill. I've struggled with motor-learning theory, but I've never gotten a clear idea of how it is supposed to work. Maybe you train—that is, you keep repeating the movement—not only to teach the energy systems to work better but also to rub the kinesthetic sense raw. Maybe training repeats the motion often enough so that the receptors get a proper workout, and, honed by use, they then become capable of making finer and finer distinctions—so that your swimming stroke, your golf swing, your forehand smash, even your legwork as you run opens up for you. (The athletic warm-up—the gentle, easy rehearsal of the movement itself as preparation for action—must be a warm-up of the kinesthetic sensors, as well as a warm-up of joints, tendons, muscle tissue.)

Let me be very physiological about this. Suppose that taking these receptors through heavy workouts does nothing more than speed up their response time, and does so just by making more of the neurotransmitter chemicals available at the synapses. If that's all it does, and if the only gain is in the speed of signal transmission, still, there will then be more time within the movement for the performer to adjust, to improve, to aim more accurately, to gather more motor units to apply more force. Practice will increase skill.

Maybe this is what the motor-learning people have been trying to tell me all this time. If so, their academic vocabulary prevented it from coming clear. I had to grub around in the actual experience, out at the edge of fatigue, before I could understand.

Stiffness is as much a mystery to me as soreness. When I duck-walked off to bed I was checking the state and location of my body parts by firing off proprioceptors. We all do it, all the time. When you resume movement after sitting still, you will move more or less stiffly until you've reestablished neural contact with your musculature and your framework. We do it more as we get older, no matter what kind of shape we are in. Earlier, I complained that when I sat still too long my joints took a set like hair that has been slept on wrong. It must be in the sensory side of the muscles that this takes place. All those receptors in the muscles must complain, briefly, when they are put back to work, dry, without the lubrication of movement.

Jacques D'Amboise, the American dancer, says that he can no longer sit still for more than a few minutes, or he's in pain. After a lifetime of hard physical work at dance (he's about my age), he can no longer endure inactivity. When he gets up in the morning, he explains, he's so stiff that he rolls out of bed onto his hands and knees, and then gradually works his way to his feet. Then he goes immediately to an exercise class, every morning, for a hard workout, after which he is just fine—until he stops moving again, allows the set to take hold. I can't tell you how reassured I was to hear him tell this story on television.

I've been reading a biography of the Wright brothers, which reproduces some of Wilbur's extensive field notes on the flight of soaring birds. Bird flight keeps sweeping me away with athletic speculation. The swiftness and subtlety of birds' responsiveness to their medium is so far superior to human capacities that it makes me wonder what went wrong in our design. Imagine the proprioceptive capacities of the peregrine falcon's musculature, the kinesthetic sense that goes with that level of performance. Or for that matter, the physical skills that let the chickadee tumble around the kitchen bird feeder, inches out of reach of the family cat.

Unconsciously, I've always known that I swim because I can't fly. When I was a kid the idea of flight almost made me swoon. It was the only activity that I could conceive might be more fun than swimming. I spent my own share of time flat on my back, studying Texas buzzards, although never as intelligently as Wilbur Wright. I built balsa-wood model airplanes endlessly, attempting to nudge my personal experience one step closer to flight. I preferred model gliders, just because they flew with the sensuous swoop and quaver I wanted for myself. I lusted after soaring. What I wanted, although I certainly didn't know it at the time, was that kinesthetic experience. I wanted to use my musculature to play in the soft, cool medium that I could feel on my cheek with every Texas breeze.

Also, I wanted to fly because I wanted to see what it felt like. This is the organizing principle of childhood. The reason I wanted to ride the roller coaster, or a horse, or backwards on the handlebars of my bicycle was, always, to see what it felt like. Maybe it is the commonest itch of children's lives—to fire a gun, operate a band saw, handle the tiller of a sailboat, swallow tapioca pudding. I wanted the kinesthetic sensation. (I wanted to fire off my proprioceptors.) It wasn't just thrill-seeking, although I did like to jump off high places and ride roller coasters, as all kids do. I recall it now as the desire to rack up the experience, to file away the sensations, just so I'd know. Just in case I came across something that was more fun than anything else.

Out of the same itch I later learned to tumble, and did a lot of diving—seeking out whole-body sensation, I guess. When I drifted away from swimming, I drifted into motor racing and then to skiing, for the same reasons: swift movement, body weight lifted and tossed about, a continuing opportunity to toy with gravity and other large forces. (Gravity is the horsepower of skiing.) I was never rash about these activities, never self-destructive. I was definitely a sensation-seeker, after sensual pleasure, but I settled for small sensations. I frighten fairly easily.

I never saw this connective thread in my past until I started hard training. Clearly, I have always been a kinesthetic junkie. I used to write road tests for car magazines, which were supposed to be compilations of objective data; I spent all my time trying to say what it was like to drive the particular car. When I wrote travel articles about ski resorts, I could never get around to hotel accommodations and restaurant fare for talking about what it was like to ski the particular mountain. I enjoy writing most when it allows me to dig away at that kind of experience, trying to make it accessible—to myself if not to others.

I couldn't know this, however—did not, in effect, know what I was doing—until I started training. Sometimes I think that training is opening up my past for me the way it opened up my swimming stroke. Sometimes I think the impulse to continue contains the foolish hope that it will open up other mysteries—age and guilt and desire, as well as the inconsequentialities of athletics—with the same kind of clarity.

# ELEVEN

# STEP, CHOMP, STEP

I FELL OFF A ladder last summer. I wasn't hurt—it was a minor mishap—but the experience was instructive. I was coming down, carrying an awkward load, trying—stupidly, just for a moment—to do so without using my hands. I lost my balance, teetered for what seemed like a long time, then dropped the load and saved myself—too late to stay on the ladder, early enough to avoid any damage but a skinned elbow. It was quite a scare. I could have been hurt. I should've been paying more attention.

I was obviously off in a fog somewhere, attending to some future chore in my head. (When hauling water, says the Zen master, just haul water.) Once I started losing my balance I switched back to the present tense, attempting to deal with what was in fact going on. During that teetering time I kept thinking I would get it back, but at some point it became clear that another approach was called for. I found myself in dialogue: here, one part of me seemed to be saying to the rest of me, *you* solve it.

I still had several options—different places to grab for, different directions to jump—and that's what got me in trouble. There were too many solutions, and I dithered, unable to choose. Later, I would remember how Lyndon Johnson bragged about keeping his options open. Someone pointed out that this really meant watching your options get closed off, one by one, until you had only one left and were forced to act. When I finally dropped the load, I was down to that sole option.

I was also back in the present tense, no longer worrying about choosing the best solution. With a great sense of relief I quit dithering, tossed the load, jumped for safety. Back to you, other self—with gratitude. Afterward, I kept remembering the feeling of relief. I was so glad to hand the problem back to a part of my consciousness that didn't dither.

Perhaps the clearest demonstration of "instinctive" athletic ability in sports is the performance of the broken-field runner in football. The great ones always swear that they don't know how they do it. "Run to daylight" is a hoary cliché (and a book title), but it is also the closest anyone has come to describing a method for effective broken-field running.

In baseball, a good infielder watches each pitch. If he sees what kind of pitch it is, which spin it has on it and where it is headed in the strike zone, he can predict better not only where the ball will go if it's hit, but also what it's going to do after it hits the turf. This seems intuitive—a "feeling" for what the ball will do. In fact it is really neither intuition nor feeling but a clever analysis of physical forces. That's hard to feature; nobody, we're certain, can think things out that fast.

A more compulsively analytical infielder might pick up the catcher's sign to know ahead of time what pitch is coming, and compare it with his own memorized book on the batter. Something like this undoubtedly does occur, with some pitches, with some batters. But to do it for every pitch would lead to analytic burnout. You're eventually going to lose track of what it is you're supposed to do on each pitch. Better just to watch the pitch, and react.

Just to watch the pitch and react to it is to depend on the

right brain—the allegedly nonanalytical half—to perform the analysis. Just reacting is sports' quintessential right-brain response. Checking one's memory book on the batter for instructions on what to do next is the left-brain response to the problem.

All that quasi-scientific right-brain/left-brain stuff is old hat now, probably because it's such a handy organizing scheme. The left brain is generally assumed to be used for analytic tasks. It specializes in language and speech, mathematical skills, and other objective, specific, quantifiable areas. It is responsible for logical, linear thought; it deals with events in ordered sequence. It is literal-minded. It is Apollonian, as opposed to the Dionysian right side of the brain.

The right brain senses the world in holistic fashion. It is nonlinear, visual, intuitive in its grasp of experience. It is used for music, for perception of spatial relationships. It processes data simultaneously, which may be the most important difference.

You do your taxes with your left brain; you dance, or play sports, with your right brain—unless you are left-handed, in which case some, but not all, of these specializations may be reversed. Never mind about that: the question of right- and left-handedness makes this subject entirely too complicated. I am oversimplifying shamelessly, and I intend to oversimplify further. I'm using right and left brain as code words for ways of going at tasks. If this is confusing, for the left brain, just think of words; for the right brain, think of music—or sports.

I use these terms much too easily. Scientists will be busy for years sorting out what they already know about the hemispheres of the brain, without people like me dividing all human behavior into such easy, diametrically opposed categories. Hip-shot generalizations by laymen aren't likely to get at the physiological realities. But the metaphor is irresistible. There are too many mysterious aspects of performance that open up to fresh understanding if we just look at them as part of a simplistic right–left scheme.

I'm certain that superior athletes do a better job of staying in the right-brain mode of consciousness than you or I. They have to: that's where the action takes place. The left brain is attuned to the future (making predictions) and the past (searching through experience as an aid to analysis). It is perfectly okay during left-brain function for the mind to wander—to speculate, to reminisce. We don't have to stay with the moment-by-moment process; we can search for meaning.

I imagine that the left brain must also be the seat of indecision, loaded with anxieties about the future. The commonest goof in sports comes from thinking too far ahead, attempting to control the future rather than attending to the present. The infielder who is busy completing the double play before the ball is in his glove, the wide receiver who "hears footsteps" and plans evasive action instead of catching the football are lost in the future. Superstars seem to have an uncanny ability to take care of business as business arises, to "stay home," as the athletes say. You have to stay with it (the pitch, the movement, the action).

Gerald Ford, the wags said, couldn't walk and chew gum at the same time. It's an ancient athletic joke. If you can't do two things at the same time, you must do them in sequence. Take a step. Chomp down on the gum. Take another step. The athlete is continually expected to do several things at once. Simultaneous action is a key characteristic of the performer's job. You deal with simultaneous duties in the right brain, which doesn't need to put information in sequence to deal with it.

When you take lessons in a sport like tennis or skiing, the instruction is usually given in sequential (left-brain) steps. When you start trying to put the motion together, however, those "steps" occur simultaneously, and you get very confused. You're being asked to think of too many things at once. You're trying to perform right-brain tasks in a left-brain mode of analysis.

Meanwhile, the brilliant performers almost always learn their sport when they are kids, and they learn it the same way I learned to do flips off a diving board when I was seven. Some other kid said, "Bet you can't do *this*," and did it, and I watched—I formed a right-brain, spatially oriented mental image—and I tried it. I kept trying it until I got it. There were no sequential steps along the way.

This is not to say that good athletes never analyze, never break down motions in a left-brain way. Once you have the fundamentals of a movement assimilated, left-brain analysis can help improve its efficiency. Left-brain analysis is what you do after your swimming (or golf, or tennis) stroke opens up for you—after you have time to discern the separate elements in the motion, and gain some control over them.

Eventually, training becomes a process of continually checking out the elements of your own technique, at whatever sport. You strive to sharpen each aspect—serially. As I swim workouts I check my breathing, my kick, my body roll, arm entry, angle of pull, point of catch, in a kind of circuit of attention. Concentration on one aspect usually lets several other parts go slack. The goal is to get the entire technique crisp, sharp, efficient—and so automatic that you can forget about it.

When you are performing well you won't be thinking about technique; you're thinking about going faster, or making the shot, or catching somebody. You ask the right brain to perform while you, in your left-brain mode, attend to other business. In fact if you're performing well, with the right brain keeping all parts of your technique sharp and crisply coordinated, then to intrude into your technique with your left brain is an interruption. It breaks the right-brain focus on the job at hand.

I asked my right brain to keep my balance on the ladder while I did something else—worry about the rain gutters or some such thing. Unfortunately, I hadn't done enough training in no-hands ladder work, and hadn't put my technique safely away in my right brain where it would look after itself. What resulted was my Gerry Ford impersonation. I couldn't descend a ladder and carry a load—and worry about the rain gutters—at the same time.

The opening up of my swimming stroke was what first made me understand that the simple physical task of swimming had some complex mental aspects to it, and that new states of mind, new modes of concentration, would be required. A few weeks later my stroke closed back up again—I lost the feel for it—and I was to spend long periods trying to open it again. Now it opens and closes on an irregular schedule, probably dependent on the amount of yardage I'm swimming, and I realize it is a small thing, a minor and short-lived advantage. But I still spend a lot of time chasing those elusive times when it reveals its inner workings again, and for a few workouts I can make technical headway. When it does, I understand what more experienced swimmers mean when they occasionally say that they're swimming well at the moment.

The opening of my stroke is another one of those sports clichés. Most of them are attempts to put into words what we already know with the right brain, pre-verbally. Jack Nicklaus has nice "tempo" to his swing. (Tom Watson's is better; Gene Littler's is better yet; Sam Snead's is legendarily best of all.) Tempo must refer to internal rhythm: good timing within a single athletic motion. Rhythm, in athletics, isn't just the regular repetition of a movement, it's the capacity to bring in each segment of the movement right on some unheard athletic beat. It's a quality that coaches look for in athletes, if they never quite spell out what it is. It's, you know, *tempo*, that's all.

This is why it was so tiring to try to learn that new sports motion by means of sequential steps. The heaviest neural input for an action is required at initiation of the movement. (Turning a light bulb on and off is what burns it out. Leave it on and it'll last much longer.) If you have to send a separate neural signal to the muscles to start each segment of the motion, you're going to be exhausted before you're warmed up. Step. Chomp. Step. If the internal rhythm of the movement can take over the initiating function, you'll have a lot more energy—and a lot more time—to focus on the content of the move. Rhythm is a means of turning over responsibility to the right brain for starting all those parts into action. The right brain takes in all the data, all the requirements, in parallel, simultaneously. You only have to initiate the action.

Tap your foot to music: you have to concentrate only at the beginning, to get on the beat. After that your foot goes on automatic. You never have to think of it again until the tempo changes. Now think of a golf swing in which (by left-brain analysis) you've decided you want your hands to be two inches farther forward at the moment the club face meets the ball. If your tempo is working for you, the only parts of the stroke you should have to think about are the initiation and the moment of impact. Everything else is under right-brain control. The trick, of course, is learning how to put all that under right-brain control.

When I was in the motor business, acceleration puzzled me. Pure acceleration is a large part of the appeal in all kinds

of car racing. There are motorcycles, speedboats, snowmo-
biles, motorized gadgets that attract their own enthusiastic
constituency. Why? My reductive mind dismissed noise and
wind as side effects, and deduced that acceleration was to be
read only in the pressure receptors of the skin as you are
thrown back in the seat—the sense of touch—and in the balance mechanism of the semicircular canals of the inner ear.
How could such small sensations stimulate so much mechanical sport?

That was before I learned that the muscles are also sensors.
Now I understand a much larger physiological response to
acceleration. Thanks to muscle tone, the entire musculature
is always in slight contraction, cocked for action. Acceleration pulls on every part of the body that has mass, and thus
loads *all* the muscles, changing the effective angle of the pull
of gravity, signaling the entire system that we are in the grip
of power. Push the gas pedal, twist the throttle, and you turn
on that entire great thrusting sensory load. It's a thrill that
some of us have found to be addictive. It, too, is a right-brain
experience.

A large part of our urge to participate in athletics must be
from an affinity for that kind of sensory turn-on. Athletes
grow to enjoy firing off a lot of neurons. I've noticed that
athletes tend to like Mexican food, to relish saunas, to slather
themselves with fiery liniments. Athletes seem to like inten-
sifiers.

Most of the high-effort requirements of sports are specially
designed ways of firing off every neuron you can summon up.
The thrill in sports—even in high-risk sports such as motor
racing—isn't from exposing yourself to danger, but from the
bombardment of sensory stimuli. Risk is only a vivid little
intensifier—a psychological enhancer that further sharpens
the sensory message.

Anyway, I now have enough experience with these neural

fireworks to empathize with the level of right-brain experience that good athletes must be having when they perform at their peak. I wish they would report on these experiences a little more clearly. I've had a whiff, a glimmer. Are these experiences a stimulus to train harder? As the Zen master says, about as much as smothering is a stimulus to draw breath.

Watching the World Series, observing the twitches and quirks and nervous mannerisms of the batter awaiting the next pitch, Chris says, "That man's in a proprioceptive trance." It reminds her of the way a cat will wriggle its rear end, setting its hind feet more securely before the pounce. Both batter and cat are firing off proprioceptors like crazy, making exactly sure where everything is and how it is set before launching the action. You check out your proprioceptors by checking into your right brain. You check out your body state—you "listen to your body"—by getting into the right-brain mode of functioning.

The batter has a quarter of a second in which to pick up the flight of the ball and decide whether or not to swing. Not much time for sequential analysis and decision-making. (Step. Chomp. Step.) *Concentrate*, says the coach. Concentration is supposed to locate you securely in the present tense. When the batter steps back out of the batter's box, he's started thinking about what comes next, rather than what's happening. He's lost the present tense, lost concentration. He's slipped out of the right-brain mode.

Every time there's a new winner on the golf circuit, some pundit can be expected to say that the valuable part isn't the money winnings or the title, but the experience in learning how to win. Every tournament golfer has the shots, they say; not all of them have learned how to win. I've heard this a dozen times, and puzzled over what it could mean. Now I think that to learn how to win must be to learn how, in the pressure of the closing stages of a tournament, to hang onto your skill. When at any moment your touch and control and capacity to deal with the course can blow sky high, you have to know how to get back, for each shot, into the part of your consciousness where your skills are still available.

Of course you have to continue to think about how to play golf, how to play the course, how to calculate the odds and come up with the appropriate plan. But you also have to shut all that out, when the club head starts down toward the ball. If you think about what will happen if you make the shot or miss the shot, instead of thinking about the shot, you've lost right-brain concentration. Learning to win must have to do with learning, every single time, to think only about the shot. Learning to stay with it. You have to know how to operate in your right brain to do that. It's another part of the athlete's job that I had never considered before. I'm not sure how you learn it.

There's a view that holds that as kids, we begin our learning in the right-brain mode, and that maturation requires us to block out that method of dealing with the world. Getting civilized requires that you block out that source of information in order to learn more sophisticated left-brain techniques. You learn to shut the right-brain door. (Natural man lives in there, and you know how frightening he is.)

The right-brain mode of functioning uses direct, uninterpreted experience, raw sensory messages. To grow up is to learn to interpret, to apply complex symbolic analyses, to examine the ramifications that surround the direct experience of our lives. Elaborated that way, experience gets more interesting, perhaps, but less trustworthy. Any interpretation can be wrong. A great deal of the satisfaction that we get from

sports must come from the certainty that sports' simple pleasures are genuine. They are not tricked up by neurosis, value
systems, artificial left-brain constructs. In athletic experience, seeing *is* believing. It's when right-brain vision fades
that we start doubting ourselves.

Maybe all the right-brain/left-brain talk is only a current
fad. Before we had this neat right–left dichotomy we used to
divide the same functions between the upper and lower brain,
saying that the "instinctive," "intuitive," less analytical-
ly conscious functions were handled by that part of the
brain–spine complex that evolved earlier: old brain versus
new brain. Or some of us prefer to divide mental function
into the conscious and the unconscious, crediting those baffling motor skills to the id (you know, the creature behind
the right-brain door). We seem to have a very human need to
split our functions into a kind of physiological yin and yang;
you can trace it all the way back to the ancient Greeks, who,
2500 years ago, started us worrying about the mind–body
split. Philosophers—and coaches, I suppose—have been
wrestling with the division of labor ever since.

The problem is, nobody has ever quite determined whether we divide the world into neat dualisms because we have
two hemispheres to our brains, or if we perceive the brain as
divided into two halves because the world really is organized
into natural dichotomies.

When I was a kid I always knew that I was terribly good at
something, I just hadn't found out what that thing was yet.
As soon as I did find out, stand back. I was, on the most naive
level, a firm believer in God-given talent. What I really
wanted was acknowledged, demonstrated superiority—at
anything—without having to work at it.

I guess I still believe in talent, but now I see it only as a very good starting point. Now that I am beginning to understand the complexity of excellence—in any field—I'm revising my notion of what talent amounts to. I used to think it was a natural flair, an inborn level of skill, a higher starting point than the rest of us enjoyed. I used to think the talented individual just started out capable of doing that difficult thing that the rest of us had to struggle so to learn.

Now I think that talent is more likely a set of characteristics that permits a different kind of focus—in whatever hemisphere of the brain. Talent is accessibility to the task. I think of it almost as a kind of victimization, a susceptibility. It's like a failure of the immune system—in the sense that we untalented slobs are immune to high achievement. If you have a talent, maybe what that means is that the task itself can nail you, drawing out of you the intensity of concentration and focus and immersion that allows you to master it.

I no longer think, the way I did as a kid, that you find what your talent is and just enjoy it. I don't think you find a talent and develop it, at whatever investment in time and effort, in order to exploit it. I think a talent more likely finds you, waving this whiff of possibility under your nose, exposing you to this obsessive thing. Sucking you in. What you find is the irresistible need to explore this wonderful new realm, and you will do so—if you have the talent—come hell or high water. This is talent as vocation: it will draw you on. Or maybe it is talent as fate: it will give you no rest. That may be what is necessary for it to hold you securely in the mode of consciousness that will allow you to penetrate its mysteries.

I'm not sure about my own talent—for swimming or anything else—but I notice this about effort: it's never enough. When I started this swimming business I dreamed only of reducing the discomfort of holding a given pace. What I didn't realize is that that isn't the point at all. The point is to keep increasing the pace. That means you never reduce the discomfort, no matter how high your level of skill or superb your state of conditioning. You have to keep increasing the discomfort. I'm not sure I have a talent for that.

# TWELVE

# THE WORK

T H E R E   I S   T H I S  liquid and you're *in* it, and that's the problem, right there.  In the first place you can't breathe it, and since what you are doing is vigorous enough to require a lot of oxygen, you have to find a way to emerge from the liquid long enough to grab some air now and then.  Efforts to emerge from it are generally counterproductive to the efforts you're making within it, interfering with the careful alignments you're trying to maintain.  It's a small contradiction, but characteristic of the way swimming so often seems to work you against yourself.

More important, the liquid requires that you use physical laws differently than you do in other athletic environments. From the day we are born, every dry-land move we make teaches us a little more about using the physical laws that apply to solid footing, normal gravity, the relatively frictionless atmosphere. All that is changed in the water. Athletic effort has to do with acceleration and deceleration, mass, leverage, purchase, conservation of momentum. All those tools are either subtly changed or simply no longer useful in the water. It is fairly baffling. A lot of good swimmers don't really know how they do it.

Here is a puzzling example. In the normal overhand crawl

stroke, a good swimmer's hand can come out of the water *ahead* of the point at which it entered the water. Swimmers themselves have trouble believing this. The strongest impression you have is that you're pulling your hand through the water like a canoe paddle. You reach out well ahead of yourself, put your hand into the water, pull it along underneath your body, and take it out again just below your hip. How can it come out ahead of where it went in?

But sequence photographs of a swimmer, taken against a background of numbered squares, show clearly that the hand often comes out of the water forward of its point of entry. The good swimmer uses the hand as an anchor by which to pull himself or herself forward, and in the process drives that hand forward.

The sensation is that you grab a handful of water and shove it back toward your feet, getting forward movement from the shove: equal and opposite reaction, as the textbooks say. In fact you use the hand (and arm) as a propellor blade, and slice through the water with it to generate forward motion just as a propellor does. What you're really accomplishing with your hands and arms when you swim is very different from what you perceive that you are doing. This makes practice confusing. Learning to feel what you are actually doing, and then to modify those motions to increase their efficiency, is the swimmer's task.

You're going to be hauling your body through the water, so you want to present to the water the smallest and sleekest aspect of your body possible, to reduce the energy required to do the hauling. The way to present the smallest possible frontal area is to get *flat*, parallel to the water's surface. (It is surprising how many unskilled swimmers fail to grasp this principle. Getting flat in the water makes swimming easier as well as faster. Your weight is distributed as evenly as possible, which gives you maximum flotation, which means you spend less energy staying afloat.) To maintain your flatness, you want to cultivate a sense of balance that responds to the tiniest divergences from the horizontal. The most talented swimmers learn to ride those divergences back to the horizontal in ways that add forward momentum, rather than killing it off. Some of their subtler techniques involve the swimming equivalent of higher math.

Then you get your body into motion. You reach and "pull," but the pull is mostly with the arm; the hand is not so much pulling as it is busily sculling about in search of purchase. Inexperienced swimmers try to pull in a straight line beneath the body. This is difficult to do, and also ineffective. The hand should actually slide downward at entry, then sweep outward to a point a little outside the shoulder. As you run out of effective pull to the outside, you sweep back in under the body, bending the arm at a ninety-degree angle at the elbow, then finish with another swirl to the outside again, near the hip. Out, in, out again: looked at either from below or from the side, the hand sweeps through a great S-curve. The S-shaped stroke used to be explained as a search for still water, on the theory that once you got a handful of water moving, it no longer served as a useful anchor against which to apply more force. That was before the discovery that the hand leaves the water ahead of where it goes in.

Now we perceive that it is the Bernoulli effect—the same physical law that allows airplanes to fly—which explains the bulk of forward propulsion in swimming. As the plane of the hand and arm slices through the water, the fluid is divided into two streams. The stream that goes over the curved back of the hand (or the top of an airplane wing, or the front of a propellor blade) must travel faster than the stream over the palm of the hand (or the back of the blade). According to Bernoulli, the faster a fluid flows, the lower its pressure. There is less pressure on the top of the hand, more pressure on the palm of the hand. This pressure differential is what allows the swimmer to anchor the hand so securely in the water.

Propellor blades are precisely pitched to increase their angle of attack, which increases the forward pressure. The search for swimming efficiency is a search for the angles of attack that will provide the greatest forward pressure for the energy put into them. Since we can't rotate the hands and feet like propellor blades, the S-curve is the compromise path that ideally allows the best available pitch of the hand and arm to be combined with the best biomechanical leverage for the muscles and joints of the arm, hand, and upper body.

As the body is pulled along over the hand, those leverages vary; changing angles change the directions in which the muscles can effectively pull. As the direction of the pull changes, the most effective pitch of the hand changes. It is not easy to find the most effective pitch. The cue that you're getting the most effective purchase is the resistance of the water to your hand. But sometimes the most resistance comes when your pull is misaligned, dragging or pushing your body off-line.

In fact the force that is generated by the Bernoulli effect is always a few degrees off the line in which you think you're pulling. You have to learn to feel out and compensate for that deceptive vector. Just as you must develop a sense of balance that is acutely aware of the horizontal, you must also learn to sense the tiniest deflections from dead ahead, the perfect straight line for forward motion. You pull at whatever angle you can put the most muscle behind; you pitch the hand and arm so the force that's developed operates to pull you precisely straight forward. Finding the line that points straight ahead, finding the pitch that puts the force on that line, can be a problem. But it's worth working for: the closer you come to precision, the faster you go for the same expenditure of energy.

The principle is the same for all swimming strokes. Some you do with one hand, then the other (crawl and backstroke); some you do with both hands simultaneously (breaststroke, butterfly). You swim backstroke face up, the others face down. The kicks operate out of the same physics, although joint limitations radically change the shape of the power stroke.

Within the strokes themselves there are changeover moments, as when you switch from an outward sweep to an inward one in the S-curve. At those changeovers, you may in fact be paddling—pushing back directly against the water instead of slicing through it. Paddling adds less efficient but still useful *drag* force to the lift force of the Bernoulli effect. Drag force also drives you generally forward, but at different angles than lift force. You try to direct the resultant of these two forces straight ahead; the pitch of the hand must again be changed to accommodate the compromise. Every inch of every stroke is really a complex amalgam of forces out of which you try to fashion straight-ahead motion.

Once you've mastered the several forms of the propulsion part, you start putting the forms together. Every arm or leg stroke is a distinct power pulse, and the next physical challenge becomes conservation of momentum: filling in between the pulses, making the linkages that keep the body flowing through the water. The seductive thing about swimming is its rhythm, built of three elements: the power strokes (which you'd like to make overlap); the glide (which you need, but try to reduce to a minimum); and breathing (you'd like to slip in a breath every time your face clears the water, but that is often less efficient). Vary the timing of any element and you may eke out a little more speed—or get a faceful of water instead of your next breath.

Playing with the rhythm is the most effective way of learning where efficiency lies. Playing with the rhythm is one way you get your stroke to open up, displaying its components to you, suggesting changes. You slow down one small segment in order to understand it better, and then—sometimes—feel that change click into place through the rest of the cycle, like circuits closing to let the message through. Getting the rhythm right is the last major puzzle in grasping the physics of swimming.

Before you get the rhythm right, you will feel that there is power available out there somewhere, within your reach, but you can never seem to get your hands and feet on it for two strokes in succession. When you do get it right, every part of it drives the next part on. When you're really cooking it's as if the quality of the water changes. It gets solider, so you find the same firm resistance, the same possibility, everywhere you reach—because now you suddenly know just where to reach to find the power.

There's a new book out, aimed just at student athletes, which teaches them to treat school as a problem to be solved rather than an education to be acquired. Learning is not the point; what you want to achieve, scholastically, is eligibility. Figure out the prof, figure out what you have to do to pass the course, and put your energy there. If it requires learning, okay, but don't let yourself be distracted from first principles.

It sounds cynical (and I'm not about to defend it), but it is a very athletic approach to the problem. Athletics requires that kind of thinking: what's the shortest distance I can go to get there, what's the least effort I have to spend to accomplish the goal? Athletics forces utter pragmatism.

This pragmatism is what drives athletic solutions right down to the physics and biochemistry of the problem. It is not that athletics is really so much about physics and biochemistry, but that athletes learn to work with and think about things in these terms. The athlete isn't thinking *I'm going to beat this guy*. He's thinking, on some elemental level, about the physics and biochemistry of beating the guy. Where do I find the leverage, the purchase, the energy, to beat this guy? As spectators (I'm still more spectator than athlete) we never see this. All those sports clichés (no pain, no gain; keep your eye on the ball; stay with it) are reminders to the athlete to play the game at the level of physics and biochemistry.

The athlete's world has these two parts: the biochemistry of energy (its expenditure and recovery); and practical physics (lines of least resistance, conservation of momentum, summation of forces, and all those other deceptively simple physical laws). It is in these terms that the athlete operates and understands that world. Romantic notions like knowledge for the sake of knowledge do not apply. This may be one more source of the dumb-jock image.

But for me, the most interesting and satisfying part of becoming an athlete has been learning to work with problems in just this way. It is an attractive if reductive approach to things, cleanly efficient. It doesn't always work, particularly if psychology is involved. It's probably not all that useful in matters of human relationships. I wouldn't want to make an ideology out of it. But it does lead to a kind of ethics of the body. From the viewpoint of health-care costs alone, that ought to be socially redeeming.

BOOK THREE

THE PAY

# THIRTEEN
# GOING RACING

I BEGAN SWIMMING again shortly after I turned 47. Seven months later I went to swim camp, and competed in my first race in thirty years. Since then I have entered every swimming meet I could—most of them within reasonable driving distance of home—at a rate of eight to ten meets per year. In my first three years I averaged something like 12,000 yards of training a week, spread over about four workouts. This is no big deal—good college swimmers train 60,000 yards a week.

A workout takes a little over an hour. With a thirty-minute commute on each end, that's eight to ten hours a week given up to swimming. That doesn't seem excessive, considering what I get out of it. There are spillovers, side effects. On nights when I don't work out I tend to fall asleep shortly after ten, which has weaned me of TV news. Three evenings a week are cut out of what I might laughingly call my social schedule, a loss that is more relief than sacrifice. Swimming is a handy excuse for avoiding things I don't want to do. So far there has been no overt grumbling from my loved ones.

I've done well. At most masters swimming meets the award ribbons are tossed in a box in a corner somewhere. You check your results and, if you want a memento of the meet, go find the box and pick out a ribbon of the appropriate color. That's how casual the sport is. I started winning an occasional race almost from the outset, but sometimes my "win" meant only that nobody else in my age group showed up. I also got beaten a lot, sometimes by swimmers who were an age group or two older than I. At first that bothered me, and I would surreptitiously check the results to find out how many younger fellows (or younger women) were slower than I. But I seemed to be the only age-conscious masters swimmer around, and soon lost interest in that kind of bookkeeping.

The open-armed nature of masters racing makes those concerns a little pointless anyway. Anyone over 25 can enter in any masters events, including the national championships. There are no qualifying standards. In any given race you may be swimming against former Olympians or beginners, or both, and you usually don't know beforehand which is which. On that basis, you can't feel very smug about beating anyone. The only measure that has any meaning is your own past performance. In masters racing—in the beginning, anyway—you race only against yourself. I'd heard that, and it sounded a little syrupy for my tastes, but it turns out to be true. An improvement in your racing times is the only measure you get of the effectiveness of your training. Improving from meet to meet is a powerful stimulus to further effort.

Or it is for a while. Eventually you get acquainted with the members of your age group whose times are comparable to your own (or who are beating you regularly), and you begin to compete a little harder. You start seeking out individuals at meets, keeping track of their performances, even watching for their birthdays. You salute with relief the graduation of good swimmers to the age group above you, and dread birthdays that bring fresh younger swimmers into your bracket. But mostly you find a group of guys that you really want to beat—particularly when they keep beating you by fractions of a second.

This put me through some interesting changes. I had spent most of the 1960s and 1970s trying to squelch personal competitiveness. I was tired, then, of having that bug gnawing at my gut. I didn't like the feeling, the unthinking need to prevail. For some reason that I didn't want to examine, it always left me slightly ashamed—mostly, I suppose, because it had a way of leading me into behavior I wasn't proud of.

I must have spent fifteen years attempting to cure myself of that fever. I never quite succeeded. In response to some otherwise innocent transaction—an impasse in traffic, a remark at a cocktail party, a hard shot in a Sunday afternoon badminton game—I would feel a familiar wash of adrenaline, the hair almost standing up on the back of my neck with the need to snap off an aggressive return. I hated that sensation. I would squelch it; that's all over, I would tell myself, I don't care about that anymore. I refused to be challenged. I wasn't playing anymore.

Now I recognize that the virus was gnawing away as usual, and whatever hormones I thought I was squelching were only washing onward to other sites, generating other pressures. But for years I managed to convince myself that I could walk away from personal competitiveness, rationalizing it away so that I escaped its wear and tear on the psyche.

Lake swimming in New Hampshire, months before I started regular training, I went for one early morning swim when there was a hard wind blowing, and the lake had white-caps on it. I had little experience with rough water. I set out, and water began whacking me in the face every time I tried to get a breath. I kept getting ducked and smashed around as if the water had it in for me personally. After a few minutes of that kind of treatment—my feelings hurt—I began to assault the water back. I swam hard, pounding my way through the waves, letting myself get halfway angry, and then was amused at my childish irritation. Before too many more yards had passed I caught myself grinning again. I was having a terrific time in that roiling lake, a roughhouse swim like a boxing match with the water. It was a long session of mindless entertainment, and afterward I drove home in beatific calm. I had the sense of getting something large off my chest—without having to worry whether such aggressiveness was right or wrong. It was instructive.

I'm not sure whether I get a similar release from racing. I'd been racing for some time before I began thinking about beating or getting beaten, rather than about winning or not winning. I still find that shift in attitude bothersome; I'm not too comfortable with the raw need that it implies.

I also began to puzzle over the notion of excellence. Sports are full of mouthy platitudes, and "excellence," God knows, is one of the worst—exactly the sticky sort of motto I associate with aggressive moralists. But you can't keep trying to improve all the time—even if it's only improvement in the amount of time it takes you to do a perfectly useless thing like swim a hundred yards—without beginning to wonder where you're headed. Where will it all end? In *excellence*? It sounds rather empty.

Whatever it is, I began chasing my own bush-league version of it, and as I began to see its sources it began to gain substance. When I began to get a glimpse of how many component parts there always are to it—whether it is athletic excellence or excellence of any other kind—it began to get interesting. Training redefined it for me; I began to perceive it as a far cleaner, sharper, more economical concept than I had realized—not a realizable state, a final condition, but only as a kind of force field, an organizing principle.

After a few swimming meets I did begin to find that against good competition I turned in better performances—another common athletic precept that I had thought was only folklore. I began to look forward eagerly to meets at which strong swimmers would be present, and to be disappointed when they didn't show. I also began to post competitive times, and occasionally to win a race outright even when the other guys showed up. That's when I realized what a turn-about I'd done on the subject of personal competitiveness, without ever thinking about it very hard. I really did want to beat those guys. I still do.

It doesn't have anything to do with the guys, really. I don't want to beat those individuals; I just want to surpass their times, their performances. I *like* the guys.

On the other hand, wanting to beat the guys rather than the times—or wanting to keep the other guys from beating you—does help you acquire sharper focus. It makes you dig in. One of the better moments in racing is to make the last turn and discover that someone you know, in the next lane, has a two-foot lead on you, but that you have something left for the sprint to the finish. It gives you a quick lesson in how to go faster. It also gives you a sizable frustration if the other guy also has something left, and you can't make up a bloody inch.

On the first anniversary of my trip to swim camp—despite only a year of competition experience, and despite my rapid approach to the wrong end of my age group—I decided to go to that summer's long-course national championships in Canton, Ohio. Posted times from the previous year led me to hope I just might break into the top ten in some events.

The most intriguing part of preparation for my first big meet was something called the taper. Not too long ago a U.S.

national team performed poorly in the world championships in Ecuador, and afterward the coach admitted that the team had been overworked, had "missed their taper," and suffered for it. It's a mysterious-sounding process, and it has to be experienced to be understood.

Before all big meets, swimmers taper off from heavy training and follow a programmatic rest schedule, swimming lighter workouts, concentrating on stroke mechanics and pace work. There are formulas for how soon you back off and how much you swim, based on the workouts you've been doing and how long you've been training hard. To hit the taper right is one of the more complex tasks in coaching. Hit it just right and the tapered athlete gets a large boost of energy and strength. Bill Tyler guided me through my taper, and hit it on the nose. I swam through a series of small meets on succeeding weekends before the nationals, did light workouts in between, and came into Canton on a rising curve, absolutely wired, bursting with energy.

I also shaved down. Serious competitive swimmers shave their arms, legs, and upper bodies before major meets to reduce drag in the water. The performance gained by shaving down is estimated at 1 percent, but this figure is highly unscientific. Most coaches won't let their swimmers taper without shaving down and vice versa, and it's impossible to know which part of a good performance to credit to the shavedown, the taper, or the natural psychological boost from competing in a big meet.

I wasn't going to do it. It sounded entirely too bizarre to me, but everyone I talked to insisted I must. My competitors would all be shaved down, I was told, and of course I didn't want to give away the possibility of even a percentage point. I bought a packet of disposable razors and retired to a shower stall for a long and unpleasant job. Bizarre doesn't say it by half. Nobody told me, for instance, that for a couple of weeks it would feel as if I were sleeping between rubber sheets, or that my trouser legs would suddenly seem to be three feet in diameter. Or about the itchy weeks of regrowing I was in for.

What people did tell me was that the first time I hit the water after shaving down, I'd be convinced I was going faster than I'd ever gone before. That was certainly true. There's no way to describe the sensation. I felt positively dolphinlike, slithering through the water as if I might squirt right out of the pool. It felt as if I were *within* the water in a different way, the liquid somehow bonded to my skin. The water felt wetter, coating me more completely than it does in the unshaved state.

If there is a concrete gain from shaving down, it is more likely from improved kinesthetic feel than from drag reduction. The skin is actually slightly benumbed—those tiny body hairs are touch receptors—but the feeling is so unusual that you become kinesthetically more aware, your attention drawn to all this delightfully changed information that you're getting from your body surface. Shaving down gets your kinesthetic attention. That, and the sheer psych job that shaving provides, add up to a powerful weapon.

C. T. Branin Natatorium, in Canton, is a huge and lovely indoor pool that contains a complete fifty-meter long course racing venue as well as a twenty-five-yard short course and a diving pool. It belongs to a high school, but it is adequate for international-level meets.* The long-course masters national championships drew over 900 entries, which meant twenty-

*Swimming facilities of any size love to advertise themselves as "Olympic" pools. As far as I've been able to tell, this means there are stripes on the bottom of the pool. The only technical specification for Olympic swimming facilities that counts is length: fifty meters. World records can only be set in pools of that size, no matter the distance or the event. Our American "indoor," or short-course, season, masters or otherwise, is unofficial in the eyes of international swimming.

five or thirty heats (with eight lanes of swimmers per heat) in some of the more popular events, which in turn meant long waits between events. The long waits and large entry meant that for four days the stands, the deck, and the walks and hallways around the pool were covered with all these aging, well-tanned bodies, lying around killing time between bouts of frantic effort. Unless you're competing, big swimming meets can be as exciting as watching paint dry. I don't recommend it as a spectator sport.

"Aging" is misleading. The justifiably small press coverage of masters athletic events always focuses on the remarkable octogenarian contingent, but most of the competitors are between the ages of 25 and 45, and they are very fit. One of the subtler pleasures of masters swimming is simply spending time with a bunch of people who feel so well. You just never run into the dull eyes and drawn, gray look of physical malaise. Competitors may be groaning about the pain of training or their racing fortunes, but their eyes sparkle, their attitudes are positive, they are *vital*, in the best possible sense of the term. Physicians complain because they have to spend so much time with sick people. They should hang around masters swim meets for relief.

The range of competition at Canton was phenomenal. Joe Bottoms and Jim Montgomery, fresh from international championships—and freshly turned 25, eligible for the first time for the masters championships—were swimming against each other, churning out world-class times. There were in fact octogenarians, elderly swimmers who literally had to be helped out of the pool—but only after diving in and swimming their races, and winning national championships. I would have been inspired by all of this if I hadn't been so nervous about my own races. I felt very much the rookie.

As it turned out, I had a fine meet. I swam only freestyle,

and took a sixth (50 meters), two fifth places (100 and 200 meters), a fourth (400), and a third in the 1500—three and a half seconds out of second place, in a twenty-minute race. (All right, twenty-two minutes in my case. Twenty-two minutes plus.) My 1500 was four and a half minutes better than I'd swum at swim camp one year before.

I swim for the New England Masters, and these results got me on two of their relay teams, which is rather like picking good parents. We took a second place in the 200-meter mixed freestyle (with Tom Lyndon, Dorothy Carr, and Joan McIntyre), and won the men's 200-meter freestyle (with Lyndon, Win Wilson, and Ted Haartz). So I ended up with at least a piece of a national championship—and a medal of each color—in my first try.

The longer the race, the better my results: I seemed to have made some headway in changing from an adolescent sprinter to an aging distance swimmer. Of my five individual races, I enjoyed the 1500 most. I had the strange image that all the training I'd done had blown me up like a balloon, the air representing my athletic capacity. My job in the race was to let the air out of that balloon at the metered rate that would keep me moving at the fastest possible pace, but that would keep me from going flat until the last lap. That image could apply to any athletic event, I guess, but it seemed particularly acute to me in the 1500. I swam harder than I thought I could, which is what you're supposed to do at championships; it wasn't quite fast enough. Ten minutes after the race was over, I started convincing myself that I could go faster next time.

I came home from my first nationals in a state of euphoria, buoyed in part by my unexpected good results and in part by a wonderful hangover of the taper effect. For a week or so I found myself waking at five in the morning and hitting the floor on the run, swirling through my days as if I were a well-coordinated team of four. It's a definite high.

I've gone through a few more tapers since, and it remains a dependable peak in the training year. I hadn't known about tapering, but it's used in any sport that builds to a seasonal climax. I recently heard a horse trainer say on TV that the horses that do well in the Kentucky Derby are the ones that are getting good in late April. He meant they're coming onto their taper.

Hitting it right can be tricky. You don't just train less and rest more; it's more complicated than that. In the long, intense training program that precedes the taper, you're driving your body down a tunnel of accumulating fatigue. You want all of the various components of the fitness equation to have their metaphorical little tongues hanging out. For the taper, the scheme is to keep their recovery rates cranked up to the maximum, but to stop loading them with fresh fatigue.

A couple of weeks before the big event you start cutting back. One formula, for example, recommends a day of taper for each week of hard training, up to a fourteen-day maximum. If I've averaged 3000 yards a day for more than fourteen weeks (which is unlikely), I'd start tapering two weeks before the meet. I'd cut back 300 yards per session until I was down to 900 yards—just a warm-up—and hold that until two days before the competition, when I would go to complete rest.

Different tasks take different paces, different energy systems; as you cut back volume you also cut back intensity, doing just enough work at each pace to remind your various systems, in effect, of what's required. You want to take each muscle group, each energy requirement, up to the point of full usage, but not into any real fatigue. As I was once advised by Dr. Bill Yorzyk—an Olympic gold medalist, and now a masters swimmer in my age group—you back off just at the point at which you start to lose the integrity of your form.

In effect you are trying to trick the systems into continuing to add capacity after the load has stopped. You're after over-compensation, super-adaptation. You're turning yourself into the athletic equivalent of a supersaturated solution. Hit it right and you arrive at the big event with a kind of physio-logical running start over your normal state.

During the meet itself I am much too nervous to enjoy the zingy high of the taper. What I do enjoy is the runover peri-od, the afterglow, when I feel about 16 years old all day long. After a few days it begins to wear off, and eventually you have to go back to doing the hard work. But there's no plunge into fatigue and depression. You don't crash.

I enjoy the process so much that I use a milder version of it in digging into any big project, athletic or otherwise. When I'm able to predict the onset of a particularly heavy period of work, I'll deliberately overload in training for a couple of weeks. I'll boost yardage, getting myself fairly tired, and then a week or so before the work comes in I'll start to taper. During the run of the project I'll do only a light workout every couple of days. The taper kicks in like high-octane fuel, and I get startlingly energetic.

This may be entirely psychological, but that's just fine with me: it works. I find I can carry through the project much more easily, riding a wave of physical and mental well-being that is almost eerie but extremely productive. You can't over-do it—you can't taper too often, and it only lasts about fifteen days maximum—but it seems to work. The only problem is that you have to put in a lot of heavy, competition-grade training before you start or it won't happen.

The fitness mavens are always telling us to listen to our bodies. Unfortunately, mine is usually telling me to eat something I don't really need, or to have another beer. I get the message garbled—but then I'm new to all this. Real athletes are better at it, but perhaps still not good enough. Dr. David Martin, an exercise physiologist who works with elite U.S. runners, thinks that although some of the top athletes "have a tremendous intuitive feel for their bodies, a tremendous identification for how they feel and how they can perform . . . I wish they had more."

Martin wants runners to evaluate their running in a more businesslike manner, breaking down their training mileage into percentages of aerobic training, anaerobic, and red-line mileage. "I want each of these athletes to think of themselves as unique experiments of one," he told *The Runner* magazine. "What they need to do is to be aware of themselves as they change over time. . . . When they begin to see changes in their physiological profile, they need to ask whether these changes are having a positive or negative effect on their ability to run well."

Welcome, in other words, to the narcissistic world of the serious athlete (would-be or for real)—constantly monitoring and assessing, self-involved to the point of hypochondria. What's this new ache? What does this mean? Oh, my God, what's gone wrong now? At every significant change in my training program I go through the same general set of complaints—mechanical soreness, mild hangover, mild fatigue. It happens once every ten days or so. If it doesn't, I begin to worry that I'm losing the progressive overload necessary to continued gain; if it does—if I'm really sore—I get jittery about maintaining continuity in my program.

This craziness points out how very far I've wandered from the idea of simple physical fitness. I started out wanting to get fit and stay that way; competition was only to be a minor intensifier, a way of turning the screws a little tighter. Now I find that competitive athletic endeavor is something else entirely. I'm not sure it has any connection with fitness. I'm certainly in the best physical shape of my life, as fit as I've ever been, but I'm also always groaning about aches and pains. What's so fit about that?

Not long ago I competed in the National Masters Sports Festival in Philadelphia. Competitions were held in fourteen different sports over the same weekend, in everything from kayaking to judo. Over 2000 athletes were gathered, as healthy-looking a group of over-25 year olds as you're likely to find on earth. But a surprising number of them were gimpy, nursing this injury or that (and still competing). Cynics are always asking us why, if we're in such terrific shape, are we always jamming the waiting rooms of the orthopedists?

We're injured because we train too much, but we wouldn't have it any other way. Competitive athletics is not a level of involvement to be recommended lightly. It's a little like falling in love. Loving is an abiding, dependable, reality-based state upon which families, social structures, satisfactory lives can be built. Falling in love is an illness, a wretched excess. It is temporary, unsupportable, often as not destructive. It's also a hell of a lot more exciting than that other, calmer state. Competition is more fun than just being fit.

This is an area in which considered judgment is seldom applied, of course. I can't really judge how fit I am, not knowing what that means. I don't know whether I'm applying considered judgment about athletic competition. I only know it has been the most sustaining, engaging involvement I've ever experienced. After the pursuit and courtship of my wife, he quickly added.

I drift into the kitchen for another bowl of ice cream and, as I pile on an extra scoop, begin admonishing myself. I really ought to cut down on fats. The rest of my diet seems to be pretty well under control. I joined the carbo revolution some time ago, cutting down on protein, increasing the amount of carbohydrate in my daily intake to try to keep up with my energy needs. But I love butter and cream and fried foods, and I'm sure that too large a percentage of my diet is taken up by fats. I really ought to get that under control. And booze, too. It's only a couple of ounces a day, but it's every day, very regular, and they do say the stuff kills brain cells.

And then—plopping one more defiant scoop of ice cream into my bowl—it occurs to me to ask why. Why am I nagging at myself? The other day a friend asked (probably in reference to the drink I happened to have in my hand at the time) if I was or was not "in training." I'm sure she had in mind our high school days, when the football boys weren't supposed to stay up late, drink Coca-Colas, or do other harmful stuff.

It really isn't like that. Since I've been training I eat what I want when I want it, in as much quantity as I choose to cram down. I drink whatever I'm thirsty for, do what I want, bustle through my days at a pace that barely stays aerobic, and simply never get tired. (Until bedtime. Bedtime is whenever I choose. I usually choose shortly after ten p.m.) My weight stays precisely the same (and I've lost a couple of inches off my gut), I feel positively, actively terrific (for all my groaning and bitching), and I've managed to put myself into the top ten, nationally, in a very demanding physical sport. Okay, my smugness quotient has just gone off-scale again. I'm 50 years old. I think I'll take ten minutes off and feel smug. I believe I'll get off my back. Have a second bourbon to go with that ice cream, Jerome. Thanks, I believe I just will.

# FOURTEEN

# THE 1650

AT THE START you feel so fresh and strong that it's difficult not to go out too fast. Slowly, now. Cool it. (Remember, energy requirements go up as the cube of the increase in speed.) Stay with the field; be patient. Try to find a long, easy stroke and get safely into it, using its rhythm as protection against your own rashness. Hurry, but try not to burn too much energy doing it. *Ease* through the transitions, get safely aerobic, before you start cranking on speed.

After a hundred yards your freshness begins to slip away. Yes, your arms tell you, it's going to hurt this time, too. That's the sign that you've burned off the first batch of stored energy in your muscles. At about 250 yards you start to feel significant discomfort, and another flash of worry that your pace is too fast. At that point you've run through your anaerobic possibilities for this particular race, a stage that announces itself in the first panicky moment when you feel you may not be able to suck enough air.

The panic eases as soon as you become reacquainted with how hard you have to breathe to hold the pace. When you really start grabbing for air—when, as the exercise physiologists say, the respiratory drive kicks in—you're well into the switchover to the aerobic system. If you've come to that state judiciously enough, you can, in effect, tuck away whatever oxygen debt you've accumulated, to be dealt with later. You're going into the steady state at which—if you can juggle all the factors, maintain the balance—you can carry through the remaining 1400 yards.

Fifty-six more laps. Eighteen, maybe nineteen minutes. You begin to speculate about human mortality; you catch yourself making a high-pitched whining sound under water; you come to hate the person who, so very slowly, is counting laps for you. But to your surprise you find you can maintain. It's time to dig in and, if you're serious about this, to squeeze on a little more speed.

Upon his retirement a couple of years ago, Olympic gold medalist and former world-record holder Brian Goodell talked about the fierce pleasures of a good 1650-yard race. He recalled one time when he and a principal rival, Bobby Hackett, had gone stroke for stroke with each other the entire distance, pushing each other to personal bests. He said that their respective metabolisms were cranked up so high in the latter stages of the race—surface blood flow dissipating the body heat they were generating—that he could see a red glow reflecting in the water between their bodies as they swam.

The 1650-yard freestyle—or the 1500-meter freestyle, if it's being swum in a long-course pool—is the longest race in closed-course swim meets. There are more opportunities to swim the 1650 (sixty-six laps) than there are to swim the 1500 (thirty laps) because there are more twenty-five-yard pools available than there are fifty-meter pools. In either case, the event is the swimmer's equivalent of the runner's 10K, a kind of citizen's race. For many swimmers, winning or placing in the 1650 isn't nearly as important as just doing it. Swimming a 1650 is no big deal, a nice little workout for most any level of fitness swimmer. *Racing* a 1650 can be as demanding a piece of physical work as you will ever encounter.

The 1500-meter version of this race is an absolute standard against which swimmers have been measuring themselves for sixty years. Before 1980, to swim the 1500 in fifteen minutes was considered impossible—the rough equivalent of running fifteen consecutive sixty-second quarter miles, or not quite four consecutive four-minute miles. In Moscow in 1980, the Russian Vladimir Salnikov went 14:58.27. He's since cut nearly four seconds off that time.

That doesn't mean the 1500, or the 1650, has to be heroic. I swim these races every chance I get, and I am not heroic. Sometimes I don't enjoy the race, but usually I do. It is an extended opportunity to fiddle with the delicate balance between speed and athletic capacity, a twenty-two minute gavotte with fatigue and failure. And when I get one right— when I'm properly trained and get the pace right and have competition close enough to give me a little synergistic boost—it is a marvelous excursion into that area where my personal limits lie. I always finish a 1650 knowing something about myself that I didn't know before.

Training for the 1650 is first a matter of getting your stroke as efficient as your physical makeup and coordination will allow, and then a matter of training your body to deliver energy at the appropriate rate. Athletic principle number one: Increase the energy available at the same time you're reducing the energy required to do the athletic task. There is no athletic principle number two.

Making your swimming stroke more efficient is to a frustrating degree a matter of putting in yardage. If you take up running as an adult, you may already run as efficiently as you ever will. But in swimming, unless you were a racer as a kid (and therefore have the yardage behind you), chances are you have a great deal of learning ahead of you. Most of that learning is going to take place with your face in the water, blindly churning out the laps in search of more efficiency. The longer the event, the more important efficiency becomes. A twenty-minute bout with inefficiency is a lot less pleasant than a one-minute bout with inefficiency, as in a hundred-yard sprint. Bad technique can be overpowered, but only for so long. The 1650 is long. You want to get the fundamentals right.

Years ago I interviewed Mike Gallagher, when he was the top U.S. cross-country ski racer. We were talking about training—I'd mentioned that I'd been a swimmer as a kid—and I expressed some dismay at the brutal training regimen cross-country ski racers follow. "At least we get out in the woods, get to see the birds and trees," Mike said. "*You* guys, you swimmers, you're the crazy ones, pounding up and down that pool with nothing to look at but the tiles on the bottom."

He had a point, but what it means in practice is that you turn inside for entertainment. A 1650 becomes a very private trip, even when you're dueling stroke for stroke with someone. It is an introspective journey through your own physical state. That doesn't mean it's a peaceful meditation. In a race you find your mind frantically busy with everything there is to keep track of. You have to monitor your stroke, keeping everything loose and long, cooling out your kick (leg muscles burn too much oxygen) and keeping the pressure on your hands and arms. (In the closing stages of a good 1650 my forearms are my tiredest part.) You're trying to maintain the evenest possible pace, to keep track of where you are and what you have left, to meter out your remaining energy at a rate that will just last until the end. You're busy.

You're trying to keep your splits even. (Someone will be taking down your time at 100-yard intervals; after the race you assess your results and plan future training on the basis of those splits.) Until you have some experience, your splits will wander all over the place. If they don't, your goal was set too low.

Good performance is all in your head, as they say about any sport. Your splits wander with your mind. When your splits go awry, it is not because of any sudden change in your physical state or any variation in the gradually accumulating fatigue of the race, but because you lost concentration. A loss of concentration for five yards can throw a couple of extra seconds into that split. Two seconds per 100 yards over a 1650 is a thirty-second loss. Concentrate.

The first surprise in racing a 1650—always, every time—is how quick and hard the fatigue comes on. You think you know about fatigue from training, but this is different (and it can be a little frightening). The second surprise is that you can swim anyway. Once you roll into the last 500 yards of the 1650, you begin to learn its surprising little secret: there is a pace, faster than you really believe, that you can hold. You're getting signals—a leaden numbness, a kind of lazy despair—that seem to tell you that you're folding. That's it, it's all over, you can't keep this up any longer. Eventually you learn that those signals are only the ongoing accompaniment of that particular pace. They are its theme music, so to speak.

The truth, which you try to experience in training but can really confront only in a race, is that the tiredness doesn't really get that much worse. Once you're there, you might as well go on pressing, through the finite piece of time you have left to hurt. You somehow simply drive the tiredness into a steady state and then swim with it. That's another part that's all in your head: how you deal with it. Hello, fatigue, come along with me to the end of this 1650. *Then* we can discuss quitting.

And if it's going right, you pick up the pace. There comes a moment when your vision of the remaining distance fits your assessment of your physical state, and you decide yes, you can make it. You might as well bring it in right. And despite the numbness, despite the revolt of the arms and legs and lungs that have been doing so much of the work, you begin to jump on your stroke. You start to drive. When you do—when you've hit it right, when you haven't tied up, dragged to a creaking halt by lactic acid—you get a few laps there at the end when anything seems possible. The pain doesn't quit, it just doesn't matter; you find it possible to go faster, and faster still. What you feel is joy. It's almost enough to make all those laps that went before worthwhile.

# FIFTEEN
# FLAT-OUT

B U O Y E D   B Y   M Y  good results at the long-course nationals, I started preparing for the short-course championships, nine months away. That's when I started working with weights, and began increasing every other work load I could. I trained quite systematically and hard, guided by Bill Tyler, and swam the usual small local meets through the winter.

The short-course season started in earnest at Yale, in early April. At that meet, a little over two years after I started training and about six months short of my fiftieth birthday, I swam a 100-yard freestyle race in :55.99. This was two full seconds faster than my best time for the same race when I was 18. It would be hard to overstate the significance of that comparison to me.

I thought when I did it that that 100 was something of a fluke, and in some senses it was—:55.99 remains my personal best. But in subsequent weeks I swam the event in the low 56s three more times. It is the nature of competition, I suppose, that my principal reaction was irritation that, over the four races, my times were no longer improving.

At the Yale meet I also bettered my times in the 50 and 200 freestyle events, and won all three races (in my age group, of course). Three weeks later, in the New England

Championships held at Harvard's wonderful Blodgett Pool, I won the 1650, the 500, and the 200, was second in the 100 and third in the 50. The next weekend the East Coast Championships were held in Bridgewater, New Jersey. I repeated my wins in the longer events, and finished second in the 100 and 50, with respectable times. I was clearly on a roll, and beginning to get some big ideas about my future as an aging racer.

What I didn't realize was that I'd reached a significant turning point in my training. In my first year of real work I'd started from near zero, and had been able to knock great chunks off my times. My level of condition and my swimming skills were improving rapidly. I'd gained over four minutes, for example, in the 1650. It wasn't unusual that spring for me to pick up twenty seconds from one 1650 to the next. But now the easy gain had all been gobbled up; further improvements were going to come, if at all, in small numbers.

The good results also raised the stakes. When I started racing I didn't have any specific ambitions. This had nothing to do with modesty; I really had no idea what might be possible. What I found out was that I could do pretty well, and the moment I did, I discovered I had a large investment in doing better yet. I damned sure wasn't going to get close—after only a moderate effort—and not find out whether or not I could get closer.

Raising the stakes intensified my training, committing me to a program and a level of effort that once again changed the way I thought about all this athletics business. Intensifying your training is a tricky balancing act. You want to go as hard as possible in each workout, you want to increase the volume, you want to pick up the speed of improvement; you don't want to go flat, injure yourself, break down.

Therefore every increase in training feels like another ball in the air, another set of variables to keep in mind. As I swam I began to have long arguments with myself over the need to be patient versus the need to hurry, to push on through. I felt twisted in two from trying to hold the two conflicting purposes in mind at the same time. This never stops; as I swim, I know I'm not working hard enough, and yet I spend half my time concocting alibis, rationales for not working harder. It is an internal dialogue that accompanies every workout. Just about the only way to shut it off is to have someone in the next lane who is a match for you, and let the wash of competitive juices flush out the internal nagging. (Another refrain begins: how can he—or she—keep up *that* pace?)

There is a perfectly rational way to go at training, and it works. Training is progressive overload. You figure out a way to measure the load at which you're training by putting it into some kind of numbers—time, distance, number of repetitions, pounds lifted, whatever. You increase the load from time to time. So long as you increase, you're gaining. If you get impatient—if you decide, as almost all athletes quickly do, that you want to improve more rapidly—there are rational ways to guide that, too. You measure effort instead of load. You find a way to gauge the effect of a given load on your state of condition. To speed up your rate of improvement, you start working with percentages of maximum effort.

The simplest measure of effort is heart rate. Maximum heart rate is 100 percent effort: work from there. There is a standard formula that uses heart rate to determine whether you're getting any training effect at all. The traditional advice is to get your heart rate up to 70 percent of its maximum and hold it there for at least fifteen minutes at a time, at least three times a week. Estimated maximum heart rate is 220 minus your age in years. For me, that's 220 minus 50 times

70 percent, or 119 beats per minute as a starting point. I take my pulse for ten seconds immediately at a break in the exercise, and multiply by six. I keep increasing the pace until I reach twenty beats per ten-second interval ($6 \times 20 = 120$). I try to do all my training above that level.

For aerobic training it doesn't matter what work you choose to raise your heart rate; all that matters is that you get it up and keep it there. You have to find the work rate that accomplishes that. With a little practice you'll recognize what that level of effort feels like. Level of perceived effort has been found to be a remarkably accurate way for cardiac patients to govern their own rehabilitative exercise programs. The same technique can work for athletic training too.

Seventy percent of maximum effort is assumed to be in the aerobic range—a work pace that you can maintain for protracted periods without running out of breath. It's a training program for the aerobic energy-producing system alone, and a minimal program at that. The progressive overload, however, is neatly built in. As you accommodate to a given work load, your heart rate at that load will go down. To maintain gain, you have to increase the work load to get the heart rate back up. As long as the heart rate stays up, you're getting some training effect.

If you want more than minimal gain, you start increasing those numbers—the frequency, the length of the workout, the percentage of maximum heart rate. Gain is extremely rapid for a while, but you come to a period of diminishing returns. If this slowing bothers you, there are additional methods for kicking the gain back up again. Interval training is traditionally the next step: the work loads are repeated at specific intervals, using the recovery rate of the heart as a guide. (Try to get your heart rate up to 140 in one effort; wait until it drops to 125 before starting the next, and so on.)

Then you start training specific systems, specific muscles,

specific responses, doing anaerobic work as well as aerobic work, playing short-rest intervals (which build endurance) against long-rest intervals (which build speed), adding skill drills, balancing cross-disciplinary work (dry-land training, strength training, other sports to break the monotony) against the unerring specificity of training. And so on: there are endless numbers, endless ways to design and manipulate the work, endless complexities to explore. A small change here can conceivably reap large rewards there. (What you lose on the roundabouts you make up on the swings.) You can plunge into hyperrational madness this way, spending as much time keeping records as you do working out. The tantalizing dream is that if you could ever encompass *all* the variables, you could push yourself along at 99 percent of your capacity to improve. You might teeter endlessly on the edge of breakdown, but while you teetered—theoretically—you could rip off an endless string of performances at the uppermost limits of your physical capacity. If you got everything right.

More important, if you're able to keep everything moving along at maximum rates in training, then when it comes time to compete you just go do it. You fill in the numbers, clock off the splits according to your charts, and that's it. You have a limited responsibility. This may be one reason people get swept up in the hyperrational approach. If you don't win, you had the wrong numbers. If you fail, it isn't from a failure of character; you just dropped a variable somewhere. If you get the numbers right, you win (or accomplish your goal). You are absolved of the requirement for emotional or psychological input. It's easy (and it lowers the stakes).

I once interviewed Dr. Paul D. MacCready, Jr., the scientist who designed and built the famous Gossamer series of human-powered aircraft. I tried to get MacCready to tell me a little about the spirit behind the project, the sense of challenge and adventure that fueled that long and exhausting effort. No, MacCready said, he just needed to raise some money, and there was this prize being offered, so he figured out a way to win it. It was just an engineering problem.

This was a man who had won national championships in model airplane contests as a youth and international soaring championships as an adult, whose competitive drive was obviously as sharply honed as his scientific mind. He took on a problem that had frustrated the rest of the scientific world since the day Icarus plunged into the sea, and he beat it. He won. They gave him a lot of money for doing it. I kept asking him, didn't you have some *fun* doing this? No, he insisted, it was just a project. You solved the problems, you got the numbers right, and it all worked out.

Maybe for human-powered aircraft (but I doubt it); never for training. For all the science, for all the numbers, training is never rational. You lay on a cover of rationality to give you something to hang onto, to keep you from going nuts arguing with yourself about whether to continue, whether to kick up the pace. Secretly, you know that the rational scheme is the airiest of frameworks, an arbitrary structure. You never really believe any of those numbers, because you always know you could have gone a little harder, found another motor unit or two, pulled out another hundredth of a second somewhere. You can't escape the suspicion that if you just get out there and dig hard enough, for long enough, you'll accomplish more than those cold numbers ever could. And so you go on arguing with yourself even while you're filling in the numbers. Increase, that's what you're after. You really have to keep the pressure on your hands (and your head), don't you?

One reason training stays irrational is that it doesn't work nearly as well if you don't pay attention, and there aren't any numbers for that. Paying attention during training can be tough. A lot of sports—particularly those that involve games—have a built-in quality that helps you focus your attention. They have a way of snapping you back to matters at hand at the appropriate moments. In the skill sports, the proper response—a well-hit ball, a good catch, an accurate return—is pleasurable in itself, a little moment of reward in exchange for a moment of focus. It helps you keep your mind in the game.

Maintaining focus is difficult enough when focus brings pleasure. In the endurance sports you are attempting to stay focused when what you are focusing on is composed in large part of discomfort. It is much harder to pay attention when what you're paying attention to is painful. The natural response is to dissociate. (Call it the flip side of trying to delay orgasm by remembering baseball averages.) Particularly in training, when sheer yardage has some value just for itself, one does have a tendency to daydream, to step away, mentally, from the work. Unfortunately, that's inefficient. For the work to pay off at the best possible rate, you have to maintain a certain level of effort. When you dissociate, that self-applied pressure is the first victim. Dissociation leads to what the coaches call garbage time—precious training time wasted on ineffective work.

Most journeymen marathon runners dread "the wall," that point about twenty miles into the race when the racer runs out of readily available energy and must struggle to the end through considerable discomfort. A lot of elite marathoners, on the other hand, say they never hit the wall, and even doubt that the phenomenon exists.

Studies indicate that the average runner prefers to dissociate from the effort for as long as possible, and then, when the wall comes along, to gut through the best way he or she can.

Elite runners, by contrast, learn to stay acutely conscious of their physical state throughout the race. By carefully monitoring as many physiological variables as possible, the runner effectively removes the wall, at least in the sense of a sudden and devastating shock that strikes in the last six miles. The wall is a real physiological state, but not every runner runs into it. The runner who is forewarned of approaching distress seems much better able to handle it as it occurs, and may even be able to stave it off. The way to stay forewarned is to pay attention. Eschew dissociation.

Of course any kind of exercise can be unpleasant enough when it's stripped of the games playing we use for motivation. Exercise generally makes you do things you don't want to do very much. I am not so gung ho that I have lost sight of this essential truth. I mean I am not actually *dying*, every morning at six, to go swim 3000 yards. There are plenty of associated pleasures, and it's possible to enjoy it when you get going good, but there's a certain amount of truth to the view that continuing, mindless expenditure of physical effort is a positive joy only to the seriously deranged.

One way you continue is by convincing yourself that the training effect is eventually going to make the unpleasant part easier. This is self-deception, since the whole point of training is to keep the unpleasant parts unpleasant. Most of the internal gibberish of training has to do with negotiating with yourself over this point.

Concentrating hard—as when you make sure you apply real force on every stroke—is also not pleasant work. It smears a layer of mental fatigue on top of the physical fatigue. The psychic effort required to summon up that concentration is draining; holding it is harder still. Occasionally I get a subtle hint about holding onto it. Once I was doing a long set of 200-yard repeats, holding a certain time for each, when I somehow let an extra five seconds slip into one of them. The next one was back on schedule. Wondering where the five seconds had gone, I realized that my mind had wandered to a recent trip to the city. There I had tried, not too successfully, to resolve a business disagreement. The five seconds slipped in during a lap in which, mentally, I was still having an argument in New York instead of attending to the workout.

It is, as they say, all in your head. For several months my distance races refused to improve. I seemed to be swimming hard but I would come into the last stages of the race realizing, depressingly, that I had too much left. I hadn't gone fast enough when I had the chance. I'd dissociated: the fatigue had become irritating enough that I had faded out, thought of other things, just to get away from it for a while. And the seconds slipped in.

When my improvement curve began to tail off, I had a sense of what was going on but I was still puzzled. There has to be a finite limit to the maximum aerobic capacity that a given physical plant can attain—or if there isn't there might as well be. Once you've gained the bulk of your potential aerobic capacity, additional gains come only at a much higher cost in work. I understood this, academically, at least, but I had trouble believing I was actually experiencing it. Worse, I wasn't sure I could do the additional work. Squeezing out those final fractions would require that I get a different kind of performance out of my head, rather than my muscles, heart, and lungs.

The same balancing acts that are required for training are also required during the races themselves. Toweling off after a successful fifty-yard race, I assess the effort. I remember making the conscious decision to turn on my kick. I had been using my usual flutter kick automatically, unthinkingly. Reaching down for a little more speed on the last lap, I began concentrating on a deeper, more powerful kick, and it brought me home in fine style. I begin to imagine a steadily accelerating kick, building in power all the way through the race. But a sprint kick is very exhausting. You start tying up rapidly. My next race is the 100-yard freestyle. I determine that I'm going to turn on my kick in this one, too. But when? How early can I start it and still hang on to the end?

One of the most elegant physical problems in sports is braking a car in road racing. The driver tries to select the latest possible moment that he or she can apply the brakes to slow the car just enough to go through the corner at the fastest possible speed. You must apply the brakes as hard as possible for the shortest possible time that will bring the tire surfaces to the point just short of sliding on the surface of the track. Your job is to approach, but not exceed, these values. You can't tell when you exceed any of these values until you do it.

It is a problem of adjustable negatives, of going faster by decreasing less. You invest a little something in obtaining a certain value—in this case speed—and then you take that value and sculpt it, delicately taking off a little here, a little there, always hanging onto as much of it as possible. You don't win motor races by going as fast as the car will go; you win by going as fast as the car will go from the start of the race to the finish.

I suspect this principle holds true for any athletic effort. It may even be a definition of athletic performance. Athletic performance is a question of learning what your capacities are; of learning how to develop them to their maximum, and doing so; of learning how to gain control of them, and then to control their expenditure in finer and finer ways; and finally, of learning to make more and more accurate judgments about the rate of expenditure of these capacities. It is an elegant problem—and all perfectly rational.

If you could learn to do all of this exactly right, you would collapse at the finish—as in the hypothetical goal of motor racing, which is to have the car expire, broken, used up, as it crosses the finish line. This may be a simplistic view of athletics, but it took me most of fifty years, a few of which were spent in fairly hard training, to understand it.

Yet there is something misleading in the image of collapse at the finish line. As a kid—back when I was sure I was going to be very good at something if I could just find out what it was—I also assumed that great athletic performances were products of unimaginable efforts of will, that the breakthrough performance came when the athlete mysteriously found the inner resources to push on a great deal farther, harder, longer than he or she had ever managed before. I conceived of such efforts as a quantum leap beyond what the individual had previously done.

That's much too romantic a view. Breakthroughs mostly come in the same way as the improvement that preceded them: inch by inch, fractions of a second at a time (Bob Beamon notwithstanding). No great performance occurs without a solid foundation. The *espontáneo*—the novice who leaps into the bullring with his coat for a cape—gets gored.

Athletes report that in the middle of breakthrough performances they usually aren't conscious of great effort but of the opposite—an easy naturalness, a sense that something is a little strange and this is going a lot more smoothly than it's supposed to. The extraordinary part of the breakthrough performance seems to come not in the grunting effort but in the control, the relaxation, the calm center from which the performer is able to command, and apply, maximum effort. Maximum but no more. The athlete who reaches for too much, who is making the grunting superhuman effort, tends to tie up—mentally, if not muscularly.

The New England and East Coast championships set me up very nicely for the YMCA Nationals the next weekend, held in Morgantown, West Virginia. Unfortunately, I drove; it took about twelve hours, mostly because I had car trouble, and by the time I arrived I was on the verge of coma. The 1650 was at eight the next morning, and on my way from the motel to the pool the car crapped out again. I managed to get it to a garage, arrange repairs, and make it to the pool half an hour before my race. Without much warm-up, still stunned from the previous day's drive, I finished the 1650 a full two minutes slower than my best time. Second place. I'd have been upset about that, but the winner, Joe Berthe, swam thirty seconds faster than I'd ever gone, so my terrible performance didn't affect the results one way or the other. I shrugged it off and tried to get organized for the remainder of the meet.

I was on my way to being whipsawed. I swim both distance events and sprints, doing reasonably well in both but considering myself primarily a distance swimmer. At Morgantown (as should be expected in a national championships) one very good distance swimmer showed up—Joe Berthe—and so did one terrific sprinter named Dick Hunkler. To make matters worse, I was at the top of the 45-to-49-year age bracket, and Berthe and Hunkler were youngsters, near the bottom.

I cut four seconds off my best 500 time; Berthe beat me by eight full seconds. I came close to my best 100 time, but Hunkler beat me by two and a half seconds, and did the same in the 50—by a second and a half, an eon in a fifty-yard race. I was in line for four second-place medals. The 200 freestyle remained, a difficult race, too long to sprint flat out, but much too short to allow you to make up any lost time.

I've come to love the 200, after being haunted by it for years. As a high-schooler I had swum the event at only one meet. In the preliminaries I had held back, saving myself, and had come from last to second place in the last lap. For the finals I thought I'd just turn on that big finishing kick a little earlier, but in my inexperience I took it out too fast, collapsed, tied up completely. Nothing had ever hurt that way before; I was shattered by the experience. The same thing had happened to me—much less traumatically—in masters racing, until I finally learned something about pace.

The reason I love the 200 now is that I swim it as fast as I can go while still maintaining some semblance of form. There's the exhilaration of speed without the frantic, all-out flailing of the pure sprints. That's the way I swam it at the Y Nationals. It hurt—I thought I was in serious trouble with seventy-five yards to go—but I held together and finished at 2:10.5, a two-second improvement on my previous best. Fine—but Hunkler, swimming a couple of heats later, was seeded at 2:05. So much for the 200, I thought.

Dick Hunkler is an exercise physiologist who describes himself as "one long fast-twitch fiber"—a drop-dead sprinter with no endurance training to back him up. His seed time was conservative for his sprinting speed, but he told me before his heat that he hadn't swum the distance in years, and was nervous about hanging on to the end.

Hanging on wasn't his problem: he somehow misjudged his first turn so badly that he had to go back and touch the wall, which put him completely out of the heat. (Despite the goof he swam a 2:15—which means he probably would have done 2:05 if he hadn't screwed up the turn.) Joe Berthe, the distance man, went 2:14 plus. My 2:10.5 turned out to be a new YMCA national record in the age group.

The YMCA Nationals don't get the large and hotly competitive entry of the other, "real" national championships (the latter are held under the auspices of U.S. Swimming, formerly the A.A.U.). The records reflect that difference. My win and my record were decidedly flukish: on any good day Hunkler should swim five or six seconds faster. I seemed to have backed into a national championship, albeit junior grade. That was all right, I'd accept it. I was not unhappy about that. Besides, I only had ten more days to get ready for the real thing, the short-course nationals in Houston, Texas.

At the very beginning, when I first thought about resuming racing, I had a very vague idea about going after the record for 50-year-old men in the 1650. It didn't take many months of training to demonstrate that such records were perfectly safe from my efforts, and I've been a little embarrassed about the whole subject ever since.

The unattainability of records doesn't bother me as much as it once did. Observing the progress of my own personal best times over the past few years, I've developed a completely different understanding of what records mean. I have become very respectful of them.

The thing we forget about records is simply that everyone is chasing them, all the time. For an event such as the 100-meter dash in track, for example, there must be many thousand more or less official attempts to break the record in any given season, worldwide. As far as the record is concerned, none but the improvements register, of course.

But every accident, every special condition not specifically forbidden, every genetic happenstance and fluke of training and competition that improve the record become a permanent part of that record—almost like a rearrangement in the molecules in DNA. As with biological evolution, the unsuccessful experiments are discarded and forgotten.

So the record comes to represent the accumulated best of everyone's efforts, a veritable history of the event encompassed in one small number. To be able to knock off that number, to revise it downward, seems a much more significant accomplishment than it did when I talked big about going after one of them four or five years ago. It bothers me less that I am unlikely to accomplish that; I have much more respect for the individuals who do. Records turn out to be weighty things, I think.

None of this heaviness applied to my Y National mark. It might have been the temporary national YMCA record, but it was bettered at least ten or twelve more times in that same year at non-YMCA meets, by various 45- to 49-year-old men. It was knocked off the Y's books the next year by a good ten seconds—by a good friend, Dave Costill. And I didn't even have a chance to defend it. I'd turned 50.

Deep down inside, I've always known that I am lazy and a coward. (Doesn't everyone know this about himself?) In college I chose to study literature because it was easy. All I had to do was read some books (which I would be doing anyway, if not those books, then some others) and write papers about them. I abandoned early ambitions in engineering because of math; math wasn't easy for me. I taught school because it was the first job I was offered; I got into journalism because that job was offered next, and paid more. (I would accept the first five jobs I was ever offered, quitting one to take the next. If someone wanted me, I was theirs.) In my college years, Saul Bellow's *Adventures of Augie March* was a formative book, and its hero said, "If it doesn't come easy, it doesn't come." I adopted that cynical motto for my own, and slipped easily along.

That is, I did what came easily, what I could pull off without too much investment in time or effort—or risk. I never tried very hard at anything that I wasn't quickly good at; I looked for early success, or I bailed out. (Maybe my efforts to squelch personal competitiveness started earlier than I realized.) It was a handy formula for avoiding crushing failure, never mind the size of the victories. By middle age I had pretty well confirmed to myself that my way was the easy way out, that the difficult was for those other, ambitious people. I wasn't proud of this attitude; it wasn't even conscious, it was just a dim sense that that was the way my instincts led me.

I began swimming in exactly the same spirit: it did come naturally, I was good at it, it was easy. I succeeded easily, at least in getting to the same halfhearted level that had always satisfied me before. As things now stand I can train for an hour two or three times a week, attend little weekend meets, place well, sometimes win. Easy. This time I am letting something push me beyond the easy part. I don't quite know why.

Another athletic truism is that almost anyone can get to be better at a given sport than about 98 percent of the rest of the population, just by putting in the effort. That other 2 percent, however—according to the conventional wisdom—is filled with stars. It is where real talent dwells; prodigious effort is put forth there, prodigious skills available. It is the realm of sensorimotor geniuses. I've never inhabited the regions of the 2 percent at anything, in sports or anything else, God knows, and never will. Until now I never allowed myself to aspire.

Something about swimming is so personally suited to me, so fitting, that it has made me open up to the risk. For some reason I am willing to fail at swimming. (Maybe this, too, is just careful selection. Going racing at my age is so egregiously pointless that failure at it is not likely to be devastating.) I've already put in more effort than I've ever invested in any single endeavor other than writing, and I have a great distance—much more than 2 percent—still to make up. It isn't going to come easy.

Frankly, it startles me that I am willing to try. How unlike me, I keep saying to myself. What's come over me? What am I trying to prove? Maybe this is a mid-life crisis after all. If it is, it doesn't feel like crisis, it feels like a standing wave, a jet stream of motivation whistling through my middle years, keeping me delighted. It feels curiously like maturation— admittedly a trifle overdue, at 50. I didn't know any of this— about myself—before I started racing.

There is one other odd little understanding that comes to me from competition. I remember when I first started skiing, the sport seemed too passive. In those days skis were clumsy and hard to turn. For beginners, ski instruction was presented as a kind of kit: you do this with your skis and your legs, you place things thus and so, and you will turn. Place your skis correctly in the snow, and the skis and the snow will turn you. It was years before I really felt I was taking an active part in getting down the mountainside. Skiing aggressively is very different from skiing as it is usually taught.

Most of the recreational sports are like that. Skiing, swimming, cycling, skating—all are presented to newcomers as simple motions; you learn to do the motions as easily, as gently, as possible, and there you have it: you are cycling, skating, whatever. I'm not sure it would be possible to teach these activities any other way. You do have to learn to perform the act easily at first. But the gentle, low-effort approach has always struck me as deceptive.

The transition from just doing the thing to doing it with the hard push of muscular force is a very large shift to make. When you do these things recreationally, you can't really believe it's possible to do them *hard*, every single step of the way. Or at least it was difficult for me to imagine that when I learned them, even when I came to enjoy them very much. When I thought of myself as a runner, when I was running forty miles a week, I still couldn't imagine running hard every step of the way.

But that is what you have to do. That, eventually, is what training becomes. Fortunately, you can make that shift in small steps for a long time—applying a little pressure, and a little more, on your legs, on the bike pedals, on yourself. Applying it in small bunches, for short periods of time at first. Gathering resolution for longer, harder efforts.

There comes a time, however, when you have to take a larger bite. You have to start trying to apply the pressure every step, every stroke. You can't, of course; you fail, frequently at first, less often as you get more familiar with what is required to stay with the effort. But you have to begin to try. It is not a physical transition, it is entirely in your mind. I believe that the moment you make that transition is the moment you become an athlete.

# SIXTEEN

# CRASHING

IN LATE MAY OF my forty-ninth year I competed in my first short-course national championships in Houston, Texas. I had an extremely good meet. I cut six-tenths of a second off my best 50-yard freestyle time, came within a tenth of my best 100, cut two more seconds off the 200. In the 500 I cut eleven seconds, going under six minutes for the first time; in the 1650—shaved down and fully tapered—I picked up twenty-eight seconds, breaking twenty-one minutes. I was tremendously pleased.

These performances earned me nothing better than a fifth place (for the 1650). Personally the meet was a great success; as far as the competition was concerned, I had my head handed to me. There were a bunch of old men there who could swim very fast. For example, I actually cut two and three-tenths seconds off my YMCA record in the 200, swimming 2:08.22. That was a full sixteen seconds out of first place—in what is basically a two-minute race. A Californian named Edward Hinshaw swam 1:52; six other fellows also beat my time, leaving me eighth. My only consolation was that Hinshaw had just come into the 45–49 age group, and I was on my way out of it as quickly as possible. This is the masters swimmer's final alibi, of course, to be used only when no other excuse cuts any ice.

But my taper was splendid, I felt great, I turned in performances I didn't dream were possible for me. Besides, before I again ran into that level of competition, I would turn 50 and join a new age group. Wait until next year, I was already muttering.

I came home from Houston eager to jump into the summer season. Good sense told me a break was called for, but I managed to stay out of the water for only a week before resuming training. I also started building docks. There's a swimmable pond behind my house, and I'd already marked off a fifty-meter stretch. The summer races would all be long-course, in fifty-meter pools. I installed small docks at each end, complete with walls against which to do racing turns, so I could swim regulation long-course laps in my backyard. For the summer, anyway, I could train at home.

I had several other training experiments in mind, not the least of which was a sizable increase in yardage. The really spectacular performances in masters swimming are posted by people who are rumored to swim 6000 or 7000 yards a day. I planned to see what that kind of yardage could do for me. But I wanted more than that. (I once heard of a runner known to his friends as Joe "Never Enough" Smith. I thought this was amusing at the time.) I went back to the weights for strength training. I even started running a little now and then, just for a different kind of cardiovascular work.

I also started fiddling with my stroke. Some of my competitors who swam so fast were a lot bigger and stronger than me, but some of them were smaller; they had to be more efficient in the water than I was. They obviously knew things about swimming that I didn't know. I was determined to learn. I started taking my stroke apart, trying new things.

Summers get busy around my house anyway. Even after I digested the idea of increased yardage, I still had the problem

of scheduling it. I could do 1500 meters in the morning—
great swimming, with the pond cool and the morning air
fresh. I usually tried to do a full 3000 of interval work at noon
(an advantage of working at home). I'd do whatever I felt like
when I knocked off for the evening—from 500 to 1500. The
Valley Swim Club was meeting three nights a week, so I
swam less yardage during those days. Weight workouts were
three mornings a week, and I had to back off the swimming
on those days too. There were some 7000-meter days in
there, but there were more 4000-meter days.

I don't mean to imply that this schedule was all drudge
work. To tinker with your stroke you have to slow down and
feel for subtle changes. You play around with timing and
movements and everything else you can successfully monitor,
and "play" is the appropriate word. I was not pounding out
every single meter of every single workout at a very high level
of effort. I approached a lot of workouts with a less than ur-
gent sense of pressure.

In fact I've almost always enjoyed going for a swim outdoors on a nice summer day, and I tried not to let workout
pressures destroy that enjoyment. For example, the pond gets
warm in late summer, and it is not water you'd want to drink.
As I swam my laps I'd get very dry. It seemed a good idea to
put a cold can of beer on the end of one of the docks. I mean I
wasn't guzzling the stuff, I'd just have a quick hit every second or third set, to keep my throat moistened. But somehow
this solution melted the high-pressure seriousness right out
of the endeavor.

The first meet of the summer was a small community affair
on Long Island. It was a long drive, but it was a chance to
visit and race with Jim Johnsen, and to spend some time with
Dick Guido, the advertising executive I had met at swim
camp, who put me up. The weather was spectacular; it was a

well-run meet; I was very nicely entertained by both the Johnsens and the Guidos. It was an enjoyable weekend except for the fact that in the swimming races, I stank. My times ballooned back up nearly to swim-camp levels. I swam hard and everything felt right, but I couldn't seem to get moving through the water. I was a little annoyed.

Oh, well, one swallow maketh not, et cetera. I paddled on in my now lukewarm pond, trying new ways to get a grip on the water, counting up empty meters and convincing myself that I was getting some good out of them. A week later there was a larger meet, at Brown University's indoor fifty-meter pool. My performances were slightly better but still depressing. I was a full minute off my best 1500 of the summer before.

One fellow who beat me soundly in the 1500 was a visitor from the Midwest with no one to count laps for him, so I volunteered. We talked afterward, when I was rather glum about my performance in general. He asked about my training. I mentioned weight training; he assured me that from his experience weights would eventually help, but not for several months. Aha! Maybe *that* was my problem.

There was no real change throughout the late summer and fall. I swam badly at another small long-course meet, attended the National Masters Sports Festival in Philadelphia and swam a little better there, decided not to attend that year's national long-course championships in Portland, Oregon. I would turn 50 in November, and needed no further competitive bruisings from 45 year olds in the interim. Better I stay home and *really* train for my upcoming new age group.

I kept up the extra yardage as long as the pond was swimmable and then, when fall forced me indoors, picked up the weight training. Gradually, everything began to go sour on me. I couldn't repeat sets that I'd handled easily in the spring, couldn't seem to gain an inch or a fraction of a second. The technique work had mostly confused me, and I could neither recapture my old stroke nor groove a new one. Everything was a little off. I felt creakingly slow. The only remedy I could think of was to train harder.

In September and October I ploughed through a long and intense project in my work, and finally shipped it off. That freed up a little more time, so I started back to the Northampton Y in the mornings, doing two-a-day workouts three times a week, getting my yardage back up. On November 6, the day before my fiftieth birthday, I did 7000 yards, almost all of it at a good pace. I followed that with a rare 25,000-yard week, which left my shoulders so sore that I had to knock off for a couple of days. But I picked the pace back up again when the soreness went away.

The big meet of the winter—and my first meet in the 50–54 age group—was at Harvard in mid-December, and I really wanted to put up some good times there. I planned a mini-taper, backing off training five days before the meet and getting some rest. I went to Cambridge with high hopes. Harvard's pool is so spectacularly good and fast that everyone gets up for those meets, and I was really looking forward to a big weekend.

It was the most depressing two days I've had as a swimmer. It was as if I was swimming in molasses, overpowered by the water itself. I felt disoriented, out of it, vaguely angry. I won some races, but only because not much competition showed up in my new age group. My times were so slow that I was embarrassed.

I had slipped back a full year, somehow losing all the gain I'd accumulated throughout the very successful previous winter and spring. I came home with a splitting headache, immediately came down with the flu, and spent four days in bed. I hadn't spent a day in bed in ten years. By the time I felt like getting up again, I threw up my hands in disgust, and packed it in until the new year.

In the late summer period, what I thought was happening was that I'd reached some kind of athletic plateau. I'd never experienced that before, but every athlete hits one now and then, stuck at a level of achievement or conditioning or strength, unable to break through to a next range of improvement.

Logically, you break out of a plateau by changing something. A plateau is a sign that you've stopped overloading: all your systems have adapted to the work load you're giving them. To get off the plateau, change the loading—or the relationship of loadings, or the timing, or the frequency, or some other training variable—so that the systems have to adjust to the difference.

This is the exercise physiologist's explanation of the plateau and its cure. The exercise physiologist is not generally driven by fear of letting slip away some dearly won particle of gain. More important, the exercise physiologist is seldom calculating these changes on the basis of a competition schedule that requires a peak on a given date. For the athlete, missing that date—for injury or illness or just the staleness of a plateau—can waste a calendar year out of a very finite athletic career. Plateaus are more complicated for athletes than they are for exercise physiologists.

There is also the haunting possibility that what feels like a plateau is in fact only "time-in-grade": a sufficient period of training at a given level of performance to nail down adequately all the capacities and skills that underlie that performance level. It takes time to bring all the systems to a point at which they can work together properly.

But my summer problem was neither time-in-grade nor plateau, and my program that autumn just made things worse. I was overtrained and didn't know it.

Overtraining is an actual disease, although few doctors would be likely to diagnose it. A version called Olympic flu makes sports-page headlines every four years, when it threatens to prevent about half the assembled athletes from competing in the Games. It is just another training phenomenon. An athlete at the peak of preparation for competition is an athlete on the brink of breakdown. By definition he or she is at the end of a carefully orchestrated dosage of maximum physiological stress. Any additional stress—even travel, or a foreign setting—can be the overload that makes all come tumbling down. Stage three of Selye's General Adaptation Syndrome kicks in: exhaustion.

Immune systems are overwhelmed; bugs that the constitution would otherwise ignore become virulent; Olympic flu rages through the troops. Fire the coach. Sports journalists can easily convince themselves that the East Germans have developed a pill that will set world records, but can't believe that overtraining can make an athlete sick. Sports journalists usually don't know very much about athletics.

Overtraining first manifests itself in disturbed rest and an elevated resting pulse rate, particularly upon waking in the morning, that indicates incomplete recovery from the last training session. Irritability, loss of weight, unusual soreness, a general feeling of staleness also can indicate overtraining. (The last was the only specific symptom I noticed in myself.) There can be peculiar little physical flare-ups of the gums, cuticles, skin. The cure is rest, and that's where the problem lies. The athlete has just invested a great deal of time and effort to reach peak condition, and the idea of resting means letting all that work slip away.

The same fear underlies the athlete's traditional difficulty in dealing with injuries—and can help explain the remarkable recoveries that athletes so often make. The injured athlete is swept with a panicky sense that all that training is on its way down the tubes. Good training is a kind of cumulative roll, a sweeping momentum that continues to build as the days and weeks add up. (As I was experiencing the previous spring.) To break that momentum for complete rest can be a desolating experience. The confidence that is so important to the athlete's success can be broken with it.

It would be less than candid not to mention the fact that as all this was going on, my professional life was in the same shambles as my swimming performances. The large project I had shipped off at the end of the summer, on which a good part of the year's income depended, did not, as they say, work out. That would have been bad enough, but circumstances kept this information from me—I couldn't break loose any answers about the project—from September until early December. At the same time I was pounding myself into human pemmican with training, I was also hanging by my fingernails over whether I would be paid for the previous six months' work. Meanwhile another big project, which would have provided a hefty year's income, teetered on the brink and then collapsed just at contract-signing time. In the freelancer's life these periods come with the territory, and I don't relate them in a bid for sympathy. (It all worked out.) But I did have some significant sources of stress other than swim training at the time. They made a considerable contribution, I'm sure, to the crash with which I ended the year.

The silly thing is that the crash caught me so by surprise. In retrospect I am amazed at my insensitivity to my own physical state, over several months, in the face of a perfectly obvious chain of events. (Say that again about listening to my body, will you?) I am amazed that I never quite saw my own transparent panic reaction—in the form of 7000-yard days—to my fiftieth birthday. I am still amazed that the cumulative effect of overtraining showed up so graphically in my swimming times, when everything seemed exactly the same.

I am also still amazed that for so many years I could have studied and written about the training effect, and the role of stress therein, without really ever thinking much about overtraining. Or that while I was perfectly comfortable reciting the symptoms of and mechanisms for overtraining, I wasn't able to recognize them while they were happening to me. He who has himself for a trainer may have a fool for an athlete.

Stress is a confusing concept, at once the cause and the disease itself, and most definitions tend to cloud, rather than clarify, the subject. I knew I was under considerable psychological stress, and I knew that the products of that stress were various changes, hormonal and otherwise, that were tough on the system. I thought that I could deal with that, that I could be tough mentally, that I would just soldier on through whatever momentary bad patch I happened to be in. I simply wasn't going to give in to stress. A firm believer in recreation, my grand plan to deal with psychological stress was to escape it from time to time in the cleansing and restoring powers of good hard physical work.

What this simpleminded approach overlooks is that good hard physical work is also stress. Training is controlled stress. The body's reaction to physical stress is the same as it is to emotional stress. Mental stress *is* physical stress. You don't erase stress by erasing anger or anxiety. Stress makes chemical changes. Refusing to give in doesn't stop the chemical changes. You can't refuse to give in to chemistry.

December, then, was a fairly bleak month. The plan had

been to start off my fifty-first year with a solid base of high volume and physical sharpness. Instead I was in bed, in debt, in the pits, horribly depressed, feeling as if I were struggling back from a serious illness—and in some low-grade sense I may have been.

A large part of the depression had to do with betrayal. Training had been a conversion experience for me, and I'd spent three years relishing the rising curve, glorying like a miser in the accumulating gain. I started the whole process with only a paper understanding of its workings, but the real experience, week by week, had far outstripped anything I'd read about in the literature. Somehow I'd overlooked, in that literature, the part about how it could all come to a crashing end. It felt like being fired from a job for trying too hard. My feelings were hurt. It was as if I didn't quit training, I got kicked out.

## SEVENTEEN
# HIGH TECH

AFTER THE HOLIDAY season, I started swimming again. My plan was simply to go back to square one: I would swim moderate distances at a moderate pace until I'd rebuilt my aerobic base. When I was comfortable doing that, I would go back exactly one year in my log and begin repeating the workouts that worked so well the previous spring. Better to rely on successful old workouts, I thought, than to try to dope out a new approach. It was all those new approaches that had gotten me into trouble in the first place.

In other words, I was chopping off variables, hoping to be a little more scientific about my training this time. In fact, I planned to make a pilgrimage to a sports science lab. David L. Costill, Ph.D., director of the Human Performance Laboratory at Ball State University in Muncie, Indiana, was the man I wanted to go see. He's the best. He was among the first sports scientists in this country to explore the differences in muscle fiber types, and has done seminal work in muscle glycogen storage. He developed techniques for measuring fluid loss during prolonged exercise, and established the first coherent standards for prevention of heat injuries during distance running (saving lives in the process).

He's explored glucose and fat metabolism, and revealed

the role of caffeine in delaying exhaustion of glycogen supplies in the muscle. He's done pioneering work in rehabilitation after knee surgery, in muscle trauma from marathon running, in dealing with the problems of diabetic athletes. Pick up any modern textbook in exercise physiology and you'll find Costill's name sprinkled liberally through the footnotes of most chapters; he's published basic work in nearly every aspect of the subject. I had used his expertise liberally in an earlier book on sports performance, and we'd kept in touch.

There's one other thing that should be mentioned about Costill's productivity in sports science: he's done it all as a practicing athlete. He's been a marathon runner for years, and he never puts an athlete through any test without trying it on himself first. His first lab, in effect, has always been his own body.

I'd heard from Dave the summer before, just about the time I started building docks. He was on his way to the Netherlands for the summer to do more muscle research. He knew I had been involved in masters swimming for a while, and sent a note to say he was swimming too. He'd had running injuries and started swimming to stay in shape, and then, in the traditional progression, decided to give masters competition a whirl. (He'd been a swimmer in college.) He was 47, I was then 49, so there was the amusing possibility that we might someday compete against each other.

In the mail from Holland came somewhat wistful training details, as Dave worked out by himself in a frigid Dutch pool, preparing for the upcoming long-course national championships. We swapped workout schedules. I bitched about my puzzling stagnation, Dave bitched about sixty-five-degree water. There wasn't much mention of science. Then Dave came home and, with no warm-up meets and extremely limited preparation, went to his first nationals as a masters swimmer. He proceeded to win the 200-meter butterfly, and swam some remarkable times in several other events. It then began to dawn on me that he must be turning his prodigious talents as a sports scientist to swimming.

That's how I found myself attempting to sprint across Ball State's diving pool with a cable tethered to my waist. The cable was attached to a Bio-Kinetic Swim Bench, a device for measuring muscular force generated. The swim bench is a fairly standard dry-land training tool: the swimmer lies on the bench, pulls on cables against a pre-set resistance, and a dial reads out the work being done, in watts generated. Costill and his colleagues mount a specially modified swim bench at poolside and attach the cables to a belt at the swimmer's waist. He or she sprints as hard as possible across the pool, and the force produced appears on the dial.

Swimming in harness feels a little like swimming uphill— you churn up a lot of water but don't go anywhere very fast. To put me at ease with the unfamiliar procedure, Costill had also suited up, and demonstrated, cranking off a couple of fast trips across the pool before I got into the water. Or maybe, I thought, he did this simply to make sure the equipment was working properly. Then as I watched him precede me through most of the other tests, I realized that he was also busily checking out his own results. Many of his tests show how training is progressing, and he's keeping a pretty complete book on himself. This was my first real glimpse of the scientist-athlete at work—and of the competitive fire that Costill brings to both tasks. The point was made more clearly as he proceeded to produce roughly 50 percent higher values than I could manage on any of his tests. Familiarity with the equipment, I rationalized.

Wattage generated is only the first piece of information developed by the tethered swim. Costill has rigged the swim bench to a strip chart, so every stroke is charted graphically: the height of the curve, the distances between power pulses, the differences between right and left arm stroke are all significant indicators of swimming efficiency. The chart gives a crude graphic representation of the effectiveness of stroke technique—which, in swim coaching, is an area of great frustration. The coach can describe technical refinements to the swimmer but can't tell how well the corrections are being carried out, since stroke technique is put into effect underwater. Costill's modified swim bench can provide a rough objective measure of the effectiveness of technical coaching.

(The modified swim bench promises a more effective teaching tool for the future. Costill videotapes the underwater portion of the swimmer's stroke. Eventually the videotape could be calibrated with the strip chart. Power pulses of the stroke could then be matched with arm position in the water, so the swimmer could pinpoint specific flaws in his or her stroke. More about videotaping later.)

Costill's high-tech approach to swim training involves a lot more than the tethered swim. Over the past two years he has worked closely with the Ball State men's swimming coach, Bob Thomas, to develop a battery of tests that keep careful tabs on the team's level of condition, strength, state of training. Swimmers are tested at several points during the season, as they taper and peak for big events. Dry-land power output is compared with tethered swim power output, total yardage is broken down into aerobic and anaerobic work, the training intensity of each workout is graded. Changes in objective measurements—and swimming times—are compared with total yardage, percentage of effort in recent workouts, percentage of aerobic versus anaerobic work, and so on. A vast array of data is being collected.

There's too much data, in fact. "I can provide Bob with his swimmers' arm lengths, or the lengths of their ears, for that matter—and a lot of the testing that goes on in swimming is of that quality," Costill says. "It has no relevance to performance." His program is aimed at finding just which data show performance change.

It's a fertile area. Most of Costill's research (like a high percentage of swimming competition) now has to do with the anaerobic portion of athletic effort. Over the past couple of decades, the bulk of exercise research has concerned aerobic function; not much is known about the anaerobic side of the equation, Costill says.

His challenge is to be ingenious enough to devise ways to do science there. Dave Costill is a very ingenious guy, and the new technology is playing right into his hands. He's using computer analysis, for example, for everything from monitoring athletes' blood chemistry through the season to managing the mountains of data generated by a teamful of swimmers racking up thousands of yards of training per day.

To round out the picture—and because Costill is using himself as a first subject, and is a masters swimmer—he is now gathering similar figures from a group of masters swimmers for a longitudinal study of older athletes. That's what put me in the pool with the wires attached: I'd volunteered as a subject, in hopes that one healthy by-product would be an explanation for, and guidance out of, my spell of athletic staleness.

The procedure was simple enough. I was ushered through a fairly standard set of measurements—height, weight, blood pressure, resting pulse rate, percentage of body fat (skin caliper method). I did a series of static tests on a dryland swim bench, establishing what was laughingly referred to as a power curve. ("You're a distance swimmer, not a sprinter," Dave kept saying. Sprinting is almost totally a function of power.) We went to the pool for the tethered swim. The diving pool was used because it has underwater viewing windows; after the bench test Dave's crew videotaped my stroke. I was also timed in a series of all-out twenty-five-yard sprints, to establish a base sprinting speed against which to compare the power generated on the bench. ("Definitely a distance swimmer," Dave sniffed, again, at my sprint times.) Then we adjourned to the lab, where I studied videotapes while the lab began comparing my vital statistics with my power output and my swimming history. Blood lactate and acidity measurements would be added to the computations later.

In the afternoon we went back to the pool, where I joined Dave and some other swimmers in their afternoon workout. My warm-up was a little different, however. Starting cold, I was to swim a 200-yard freestyle sprint at exactly 90 percent of my best time for that event; immediately upon finishing, an electrocardiogram was strapped to my chest to record heart rate and recovery, and I was punctured for the blood chemistry studies.

Swimming the 200 at 90-percent velocity was not easy, even with pace lights on the bottom of the pool. The lights were set for an even pace, so the first couple of laps (of eight) were fairly leisurely. As I began to tire, however, it was as if the lights were accelerating, trying to run off and leave me. It became a dogged game of catch-up through the last six laps, and I finished with my tongue hanging out. An even pace turns out to be a very unpleasant way to swim the 200.

All of my results—in strength, power, and speed—were woefully short of the kind of performance that Costill was accustomed to measuring, of course, but then so are my swimming times woefully short of decent contemporary college performances. (Or high school or junior high performances. Swimming is evolving explosively: Mark Spitz's 1972 Munich world records wouldn't have gotten him into the tryouts for the 1984 U.S. Olympic team.) But there were no anomalies, no glaring high or low points in the record, pointing up specific training lapses or overcompensations. I just needed to get back in shape.

There was no immediate specific gain for me as a swimmer from the high-tech portions of the testing program, except for the checkup function. I was only contributing numbers to an ongoing study which should, over time, provide some new insights into training methods and the coaching of swimming technique.

But the videotaping was another matter, immensely valuable to me. I had a chance to study the tape, stop it at any point, back it up, advance it a frame at a time, see exactly what I was doing underwater at any point in my stroke. I even reviewed it with Coach Thomas. I was appalled. The technical errors were immediately apparent.

I'd been taped before, at swim camp, but only above water. I was struck once again by how what you're doing looks so different from what it feels like you're doing. I found I was doing things I explicitly thought I was avoiding, and neglecting to do things I thought I'd grooved long ago. I was "laying on my arms"—pushing down on the water instead of pulling myself through it. I was dropping my elbows, thereby losing the use of my forearms as a pulling surface. I was cutting my stroke short, giving away the last (and most powerful) 15 to 20 percent of the power pulse. So in addition to figuring out what had gone wrong with my training, I now had another job ahead of me: learning how to swim again.

I've left out part of this story. When I was corresponding with Dave in the Netherlands, I was struggling to master a new word processor, so he knew I had access to a computer. A few weeks before I visited Ball State, I received in the mail from Costill several pages of computer printout, the first line of which read "PRINT 'SWIMMING WORKOUT EVALUATION.'"

It was gibberish to me—I'm no programmer—but I fed all those mysterious symbols onto a floppy disk, and lo, I had my own swimming workout evaluation program. After each workout I feed pertinent data about yardage, pace, and interval times into the machine, and get several interesting numbers. Each set that I've swum is evaluated for swimming velocity (as a percentage of maximum speed) and swim-to-rest ratio. (Swim-to-rest ratio is a rough index of where the work falls on the progression from aerobic to anaerobic exercise. The higher the ratio, the more aerobic the work.) The workout as a whole is rated for swim-to-rest ratio, and total yardage, total interval yardage, and average percentage of sprint speed are also calculated.

These data are also incorporated into a single overall rating of the training intensity of the workout, which is the most interesting figure of all. Training intensity is calculated from a formula that considers all of the above data, plus the average amount of daily quality yardage for the swimmer for the preceding two weeks, in order to insure a progressive work load. Percentage of swimming velocity has been given a slightly heavier mathematical value than the other factors, its weight keyed to careful measurement of blood lactic acid produced by swimming at different velocities. (That's what the 200 at 90-percent effort was all about.)

The computer program, developed by Costill and his colleague Doug King, crunches all of this into a single number, training intensity. T.I. values of less than 50 are rated as low in stress, values of 50 to 80 are rated as moderate, and values above 80 are high in stress. Costill figures that a given swimmer can repeat workouts of an intensity of less than 50 almost indefinitely, with little real stress—and little training effect. Workouts rated from 50 to 80—which may include some high-intensity intervals, but which aren't physiologically devastating—can be tolerated for several days in a row without severe accumulating fatigue. Workouts rated above 80 take their toll, reducing performance in subsequent training days. After you've racked up an 80, you probably need an easy day for recovery.

Once I had the evaluation program on a disk, I went back to my training log, selected that dreary period that included my fiftieth birthday, and ran through a couple of weeks of workouts. The day before my birthday I'd done a workout with a training intensity of 117; the next day's effort rated 121. There was one period—not too long before I crashed and got sick—of nine workouts in a row with an average training intensity of 85.3. Most of my high-intensity workouts were high in yardage rather than speed, but the evidence was plain as day, once I had the computer program to pull the various volumes and values together for me. No great mystery: I simply needed rest. It was reassuring to have the computer confirm what my swimming times had finally managed to tell me the previous fall. Maybe next time, with the help of the computer, I would get the message a little earlier.

My adventures as a 50 year old, toying with some high-tech gadgetry and letting scientists take my modest measurements, don't have a great deal to do with the advancement of sports science. But the siege of athletic staleness that sent me in search of answers is very much the kind of training result that is the subject of contemporary sports research. We know quite a bit about training people up to one-time peak performances. The problem is maintaining: consolidating gains, organizing training over consecutive seasons, planning tapers, bringing whole teams along in concert. The long-term stuff is highly complex, mysterious, subjective. What Costill is seeking are ways to teach swimmers not only to swim faster, but also to maintain that speed over the long season, and to increase it precious fractions more for the most important competitions.

The problem, according to Costill, is our huge body of incompletely absorbed, dimly understood experience in training. "Training programs have already evolved," he says, "and rather than try to design a totally new one, the smart coach is going to go with one that is already succeeding. Nobody is going to try a radically different training program.

"Most training is intuitive. The coach may slightly modify what he's done in the past. He may have kept some records of what worked and what didn't. But not many coaches are very systematic about it. Next year they're liable to do pretty much what they did last year. Most coaches, hell, there's no way they could go back and look at what they did last year. You ask them what they did in training the first week of January last year, and they won't have a clue.

"So when I look at training programs and see things that aren't what I would recommend, my impulse is to dive in and try to find out why it works, and how it could be better. That's basically all I'm trying to do."

All athletic training can be placed somewhere on a scale of zero to 100 percent, whether the percentage is of maximum speed, effort, intensity, volume. All other things being equal, the athlete who trains hardest—closest to 100 percent in all measures—will perform best. Unfortunately, training is stress, and when stress gets too high, the organism stops improving and starts breaking down. Too high is somewhere less than 100 percent. (If it weren't, training would be easy to plan, if hard to do.) The goal is to find where, on that hypothetical zero-to-100 percent scale, the maximum gain can be maintained. The evidence suggests that your best results should come from holding somewhere close to a golden mean of about 70 percent in training values. But if you are, and someone else is holding to 71 percent, does this mean you get beat? It is the essential puzzle of athletic training. It is where some of the most promising work in sports science is now going on.

Dave Costill isn't necessarily trying to discover whether 70 percent is the proper figure; he *is* trying to measure the 70 percent. He's trying to help the athlete know when he or she is operating at 70 percent, when at 71 percent, when at 69 percent. He is trying to develop more concrete markers than, say, perceived effort, to guide the athlete through the delicate balancing act that is serious training.

When he measures blood lactates, he is gathering the bits of intelligence that will help more accurately to measure intensity of effort, that will predict recovery times and maximum work loads. When he compares dry-land bench and tethered-swim power production, he is developing a tool for gauging future training states. When he computerizes workout data, he is providing a record that helps the athlete more intelligently judge his or her own future plans. He is, in short, gathering up the tiny pieces of information that will help the athlete to accrue the fractions of gain out of which superior performances are always built.

Costill is trying to systemize things. "What science tries to do is put things in order, to tag things so that you can keep track of them, to find out what is actually happening. My goal, in all sports-related research, has always been very clear-cut. The ultimate goal is to be able to help the athlete to perform better by reducing error in technique, or to optimize his physiological potential."

It's as simple as that. All you have to do is find the places—in among the molecules and bioelectrical minutiae of the athletic physiology—to hang the tags. Dave Costill is very good at tag-hanging.

I came home buoyed immeasurably, reassured that my training was once again on course, the mysteries of the previous fall's sputtering collapse all solved. And besides, I had this new stroke to learn. Ten days after my visit to Muncie, I swam in a small local meet. In a six-minute race—with video images filling my head—I cut about twelve seconds off the times I'd been consistently swimming throughout the fall and winter. I don't know if it was the rest, the technical sharpening, or just the psychological boost from all the attention. I'm not ingenious enough to separate it out. At that point, I didn't much care.

# EIGHTEEN

# STAYING WITH IT

E ACH Y E A R T H E R E is a national one-hour swim, held as a postal competition. With an observer to count your laps, you swim for an hour in your local pool, then mail in your total yardage. In late winter after my fiftieth birthday, as I began to round into decent shape after my holiday layoff, I placed second in that strange "race." With the exception of my accidental YMCA 200 victory, it was the best individual placing I had achieved nationally, and I was proud of it.

Swimming nonstop for one hour is not so much swim racing as it is an exercise in mental discipline. Ten minutes into it I remembered the year before, when midway through the event I'd sworn off ever doing it again. After about forty-five minutes there was a period when I wasn't quite hallucinating, but I was imagining that the pool was in Tibet and I was splashing along among 20,000-foot mountain peaks. I have no idea what caused this particular fantasy, but marathon swimmers tell me that similar disconnections from reality aren't unusual. As I said, it is a strange event. My second-place finish was curiously prophetic of the season to come.

Over the rest of the spring I worked my way back down to decent, if not spectacular, times. The new age bracket was fairly easy pickings, and I won most of my races. Going into the final spring series I won four out of five at the New England Championships, five out of five at the East Coast Championships. The latter included a very good, but devastatingly painful, 1650, at 21:16—the best I'd done without tapering and shaving down.

The YMCA Nationals were in Chicago, a week later. If I swam well there, I had a good chance to win all five of my freestyle events. I didn't. I won two races (the 50 and 200) and placed second in the other three. That's when Dave Costill won a dinner from me by smashing my previous year's 200 record by ten full seconds. I blew the 100 completely, misjudging all three turns, and finished laughing at my own incompetence. I swam my second-best 500 ever, but a fellow named Wayne Leengren stayed right with me for 400 yards, then pulled out two seconds on me in the last 100, despite anything I could do.

The shocker was the 1650, my favorite race. I was perfectly placed, with Leengren, the only other swimmer I had to worry about, in the next lane. We stayed together for about 700 yards, and then he began methodically to pull away. I watched him go, feeling only a kind of sour disappointment with myself. I simply didn't want it badly enough, which is another cliché I'd never examined before. In some way I didn't quite understand, the previous week's 1650 was still too raw in my mind, if not in my body.

After Chicago I had two weeks to taper for the short-course nationals, to be held in Fort Lauderdale. I had computer workout evaluations to guide me. It would be my first nationals at the young end of an age group. This time, I was sure, I would get everything right. But during the two weeks I seemed to have trouble getting focused. For some reason I kept remembering the 1650 in Chicago.

A friend had the assignment of following skier Ingemar Stenmark for a few days, as Stenmark went about the business of winning another world championship. There was a period of several years when Stenmark was by a large margin the best ski racer in the world. "I had breakfast with him one morning," my friend told me. "You ought to see Ingemar Stenmark eat bacon and eggs sometime. He eats slowly, he's very calm, but when he eats bacon and eggs, that's all he does. He becomes totally dedicated to eating bacon and eggs. Every movement of the knife and fork is perfectly controlled. You get the sense that for a few minutes there, he is very good at eating bacon and eggs, maybe as good as anyone has ever been at it. Of course," my friend continued, "he's that way about everything else, too."

After a long and fruitful career Stenmark has begun to decline. He's past it, the critics say, his remarkable flowing precision gone. He has begun to make mistakes. Scientists tell us that it isn't the absolute level of performance that falls apart with aging—not the strength or quickness or even the alertness—so much as it is the capacity to sustain the performance. You lose the capacity to pull things together, to bring the intensity of focus to bear.

I never finish a bowl of ice cream without wishing I'd paid more attention to the flavor while I was eating it. I can't seem to. I keep yanking my attention back to the flavor, but it drifts away again.

This failure was brought to my attention as I was listening to a concert not long ago. I was really enjoying the music, which stimulated a lot of thoughts about performance. I didn't want to let those thoughts slip away, so I began jotting notes while the concert continued. In doing so I missed most of the music that was stimulating the thoughts in the first place. The music was more enjoyable than the thoughts, goodness knows, but in my infernal scurrying busy-ness I let the music slip away. It is a childish frustration, I suppose, but I've never stopped suffering from it.

The way to pay attention to the flavor of ice cream is to plug back into your taste buds, to work the mental shift that focuses your attention on the sensory information coming from your mouth. The way to avoid missing the music in the concert is to do the same with your eardrums, to refocus on sound itself. The mental shift you make is from the left brain back to the right brain.

I'm still using right and left brain as metaphor, for the mental states required to perform what science assumes are right- and left-brain functions. The senses are one doorway into the right brain: yank your attention back to the sensory messages and for a brief period, anyway, you are able to operate in the present tense. To stay there, you have to find a way to shut out the yammering left brain. Staying there is the difficult part. I wish I could get better at it.

It seems to me that deliberately checking back into the senses in this way ought to be useful for athletic purposes. So far it hasn't helped me—not enough, not with the ice cream, anyway. As I understand meditation and other esoteric mental disciplines, many of them are devoted to repetitious, conscious switching of the mind from left- to right-brain states. I assume the idea is that practice can improve this capacity. As the Zen master says, when eating bacon and eggs, just eat bacon and eggs. These disciplines seem to regard right-brain consciousness as a desirable state, if only as a restful alternative to our more habitual left-brain mode. I haven't seen such practices described from a right-brain/left-brain viewpoint, but that seems to me what they are talking about. I've never tried to master any of these disciplines, so I'm only speculating.

When I first got interested in athletics, I had a vague sense of a particular silken quality of movement that characterizes the really superior athlete. It is a quality that we all recognize instantly, even if we can't quite describe it. I really wanted to understand what it is that is so fluid, and so different from everyone else, in the performance of athletes of the caliber of Lynn Swann, Reggie Jackson, Evonne Goolagong Cawley. Jamaal "Silk" Wilkes, the pros' own role model for physical efficiency. (Or Secretariat; these are human Secretariats, every one of them.) In the past few years I've run across a hundred different explanations for characteristics that contribute to this quality of movement, but the clear definition—the unified field theory of athletics, if you will—continues to elude me.

One characteristic that I once thought would explain everything is compactness. "He's got a very compact swing," they say, of baseball players as well as golfers. The good boxer has a compact punch; the pitcher is "keeping everything nice and compact today." It is a way of avoiding the introduction of error from excessive angles, awkward reaches. It makes biomechanical sense, just as a way of seeking out the best solution to the physics of the task.

It is also a way of keeping a lid on things. One thing that always distinguishes good performers, athletic or otherwise, is range. The great performers always have the widest range of possibility from which to select. They cover the whole field, they go from high to low, from hard to soft, they bring full force to bear when it's called for, but they will also, now and then, put a lid on it. They will take a little off. Performance, above all, is control.

Taking a little off has a physiological corollary. The finer levels of control of motor skills come not through activation of muscles but through their inhibition. Motor learning is first a process of learning to fire the proper motor units, and then, in search of fine control, learning not to. You learn which muscles not to fire; you learn when not to fire them.

To accomplish this delicacy of signaling, you have to be able to cut through the chaos of neural noise. There is a great deal of other signaling going on in the muscle during the vigorous action of performance. There is mechanical signaling for contraction and relaxation, of course, but there is also metabolic signaling, to keep up with energy production, waste removal, heating and cooling. In almost any kind of performance there is neurological noise from sensory bombardment—lights, sounds, crowds. There's also nervous tension over things like rankings, ratings, careers, which makes its own neural noise. All that can be so distracting that any performer must ache to let fly with a surge of maximum effort, just to overpower the chaos. The temptation to do that must be tremendous. To be able to maintain the delicate touch of fine control under those conditions requires a very special kind of concentration, a hard mental effort.

Or perhaps that effort is only required to get you into the performance, into the mental state in which you perform best. My assumption is that once you've burned through to the performing state, the performance itself draws you along. It holds you in the proper mode of consciousness. Good performance must always have that quality to it. The trick is to avoid falling out of that state.

And, at the proper time, to take a little off. "Relax," the coach keeps saying. (Don't waste energy contracting muscles you aren't using.) For even the most explosive, all-out efforts—lifting weights, putting the shot, running sprints—the athlete has to maintain a small element of relaxation. You have to cool out everything but what works. You can't consciously do that, of course. You can't monitor that much and still perform. You have to put away the instructions to relax in the right brain too, where simultaneity can be dealt with. You have to stay with the part of your consciousness that knows that performance isn't always just bulling ahead. Sometimes you have to wait, to ease up, to feel around in your capacities for just the right touch to make the motion work. Even in athletics, less is sometimes more. The propriceptors, the motor neurons know this. The right brain knows this. It's the left brain that has trouble getting the message.

I'm trying to learn how that works. I wish I hadn't started so late. I wish there were more time. I keep hurrying, and I'd really rather not do that.

When real athletes—not dilettantes like me, but full-time athletes—begin to bump up against the problems and realities of aging, the result is a poignant enhancement of both. The aging athlete, hanging on, has to resort to a broader assortment of skills and intelligences to maintain performance. Doing that seems somehow to ennoble the whole business of athletics. Age never seems so powerful as when it begins to sap the strength and swiftness of the great athlete; age and the athlete both gain in stature when they meet.

What's more, without the heightening, intensifying effect of aging, it isn't even possible to think very hard about the elements and details of athletics. So long as speed, strength, and stamina appear to be permanent and inexhaustible, they elude examination. It is only when we see that they are finite—and mutable—that we're motivated to try to understand them. That's what leads to my crack about athletics being wasted on the young. That was true for me, anyway. The largest gift that aging has brought me may be the heightening of appreciation of the capacities I have left. And the sweetening of my gratitude for the capacity that, through training, I've gotten back.

I haven't gotten everything back. For all my arguments about training as an antiaging scheme, aging does go on. My hair continues to whiten, my skin to sag. I recognize my own aging in muscular stiffness, in subtle changes in hearing and vision (particularly at night). No matter how sharp my physical processes may seem to have gotten, I'm still clumsy, and getting clumsier. I'm having to learn to be more careful, to stop trusting quick reactions to snatch equilibrium back when I stumble or misjudge. I keep noticing that change. Aging is real, all right.

What age specifically attacks is the range that characterizes the good performer. This is not so metaphorical as it may sound. Our hearing loses the capacity to distinguish both high and low tones: we lose auditory range. We lose short-range visual focus—and, in night vision, the ability to see clearly in dim light. Our voices even lose both high and low registers. The fine controls, the fine discriminations at the limits of our range begin to go. Everything is being pulled back toward the dull middle.

The athlete has "lost a step," the pundits say—or maybe half a step. He can't quite cover the same ground he used to. The zip is gone from his fastball, he doesn't get the bat around as well, he just can't get as high, going after rebounds, as he did when he was MVP. (That wonderful year.) The dimensions are reduced, the skills pulled in—to operate over a smaller sphere of activity. The tether is getting shorter.

Kids spend their time extending their range, testing limits. How far can you jump, reach, lean, how hard can you do this, how fast can you go? Aging athletes struggle to retain—

or regain—that range. Nowadays, the smarter ones use stretching to help resist loss of range. They stretch their frames, their reach.

There are two ways to stretch. You can stretch the way you do when you rise from your desk, the way a cat does, unaware, your body taking over and demanding that you pull things back into their proper places. Or you can stretch and think about it, taking deliberate care of muscles left half-cocked by fatigue. It probably does some good to stretch unthinkingly. I believe you do yourself more good, accomplish more, if your attention is focused tightly, if you are consciously monitoring the stretch within the body of the muscle. I think if your attention is in there in the workings of the muscle, tracing the stiffness and soreness throughout its length, you stand to gain much more. I think that you are able that way more fully to regain the loose, uncontracted state that opens the muscle tissue to restoration and replenishment, to growth. Stretching, here, is also a metaphor.

Attention is the hard part. Trying to pay attention to a stretch is exactly like trying to pay attention to the flavor of the ice cream all the way to the bottom of the bowl. It requires the same kind of homing in, of focusing, that you need to put pressure on each stroke, to find and put to use new motor units, to pull yourself together. It's the same focus you need to hold off fatigue long enough to win the race. There are differences, but they are in degree, in intensity, not in kind.

It is a rueful truth of athletics that there isn't that much difference, neurologically, between the flood of sensation from a mouthful of peppermint ice cream and the flood of sensation from a muscle on the edge of failure. Both pull you into the present tense—for a moment. The hard job is to stay with them. I don't like this particular truth one bit, but there it is, right there in the neurons.

This begins to sound like more of that mystical stuff. I'm interested in demysticizing athletics. There is a large mystical lobby in sports. Its members range all the way from the pietistic Fellowship of Christian Athletes to the terminally loopy, out-of-body, I-talk-to-porpoises types. All of them propose alternate realities to cover the sports experiences they otherwise can't explain. I don't think that's necessary. If you dig deeply enough into the physiology (and the physics) of sports there are perfectly sufficient explanations to cover even the most bizarre occasions, without reaching outside the reality we live in every day.

There are also plenty of people in sports who are more tenaciously literal-minded than I am. For them the very mention of things like states of consciousness and different hemispheres of the brain is tantamount to hiring a team witch doctor. I'm sorry for that. I think the evidence supports at least a little theorizing.

There is one reasonably common—and well-reported—experience in sports that seems to spawn a great deal of mysticism. It comes in those special moments when the good athlete significantly surpasses himself or herself: Billie Jean King winning her last Wimbledon title, quarterback John Brodie feeling he could guide passes into the hands of his receivers almost by pure thought, Bob Beamon leaping two feet beyond anything mortal man had previously accomplished in the long jump. Less well known athletes experience their own smaller-scale versions of these moments from time to time, and come away moved, shaken. Some of them have been known to convert to Christianity or some other belief system on the spot.

They have obviously undergone a powerful transcendent experience of some sort, well outside the usual realms of sport. Post-event interviews expose a curious consistency of reaction. If you ask almost any of these athletes about the experience, he or she is very likely to tell you, yes, *it really came together* that time. That expression has entered the language of sports. A modest theory suggests itself.

It really came together; I really got it together this time. There is a rich metaphor here, too. So often in sports what we are struggling with are widely disparate skills, capacities, even energy systems. Once you understand the basic skill of your sport—once it opens up for you so that you perceive its separate parts—then to work with that skill is to try to pull those parts into more fruitful or more efficient alignments. You begin to feel that that is literally what you're trying to do: pull things together.

Athletic performance almost always requires that the athlete operate from the right brain during the flow of the action. (When the club head starts down toward the ball.) It also requires that the athlete be capable of analytic thought, to deal with the changing strategies of the competition. This is left-brain analysis, performed, if necessary, in breaks in the flow of the game. You might say that the athlete uses his left brain to figure out what to do, and then calls up the right brain and locks into it for the actual performance of the plan.

There's a great deal of switching back and forth going on here. The more hectic the action, the more rapidly must the athlete be able to switch, to focus on the appropriate action with the appropriate hemisphere. Maybe when that transcendent state occurs, what the athlete is pulling together are the two states of consciousness, the two hemispheres of the brain. Or maybe when the athlete really pulls everything together—pulls all those separate parts of his skill into the most efficient relationship, pulls the energy systems into some kind of balanced state, pulls together all the conflicting demands of the contest he is in—he passes into that transcendent state. It hardly matters whether you think of it as merged left and right hemispheric functioning or merged athletic capacities. The result is the same. The possibilities of the game, the sport, the human participant are permanently raised.

I doubt that anything like that will ever happen to me, which is okay. I'll settle for a little improvement in my own capacity to stay with the action a little better. It's very frustrating. It reminds me of when I was a kid, when I was having some special treat—a roller-coaster ride, a trip to the circus. I would realize that I was having a terrific time and that it was slipping away while I was having it. Even before it was over I would fear that I wouldn't be able to remember it well enough.

This feeling has begun hitting me again with renewed piquancy since I began racing. It may just be because I'm having such a terrific time—again—in an elementally childish way. For whatever reason, the mood returns. I'll finish a good race, climb out of the pool, and a few minutes later think, gee, that must have been fun, I wish I'd been there for that one. I wish I'd paid more attention. I am still convinced that I can learn to pay more attention.

Or maybe it's just that age applies a certain urgency to my experience. To all the good reasons that younger, real athletes have for busting their humps in these pursuits, age adds one more. To become an athlete at age 47, or 50—or 90, I'm sure—is merely a way of saying, *"Wait!"* It is a way of grabbing time by the lapels, of saying stop, wait a minute, let me understand what is happening here. Maybe the point isn't to fight age off but to let it come on, to get inside it, to find out just what it is.

It works, sort of—although not in the ways I had imagined. A minute spent swimming a 100-yard race is a very different minute from all the other minutes in my life. For all my inattention, I will remember it well enough. It is made up of an intensity that the ordinary, nonathletic dailiness of the rest of my minutes can't hope to match. There's simply more life in it. This, too, is a sports cliché that has opened up for me—like my swimming stroke—and revealed interlinked parts that I never knew were there.

These parts are small truths, I hope. The only unpleasant part of aging is loss of function. All the rest of it is really rather pleasant. Here is a way of hanging onto function, of fighting its loss: with work, with training. I couldn't know that until I'd done it. What's more, I couldn't do the training without the racing to pull me on. Racing serves another purpose. A natural fear of aging is that our experience will lose its intensity. Racing—competing—guarantees intensity. It's just an organized way of continuing to explore one's limits. Doing that is always an intense experience (and it keeps the limits from shrinking).

I may not have stopped aging in its tracks—and that doesn't seem as important now as it did when I started—but I have certainly stopped the loss of intensity. When I try to assess this whole adventure, I find an interesting progression. I like what training has done for my health, although that's sort of a savings account—it's reassuring, but it has little to do with everyday experience. I really like the way training makes me feel: I even like the soft fatigue that forecasts energy restored. I particularly like the control that training gives me over the ebb and flow of my metabolism. It's worth the trouble just for that. But I've also come to enjoy the training itself, the hard use, the complex and challenging work. That continues to surprise me. Even more surprising—a bonus on top of that—is to discover that the more I train, the better the rest of my work goes, the sharper and clearer and more efficient my approach to everything else I do. I swear it. That's perfectly thrilling. And then there's the racing, the competition itself, which is simply the most fun I've ever had.

And then, from time to time, on top of all the rest, there is *winning*. Why did I wait so long to get involved in this?

My first short-course national championships as a member of the 50–54 age group presented a familiar scenario. Present in Fort Lauderdale were a very good sprint swimmer, a Californian named Donald Hill, who was three or four seconds better than the field in all the shorter races; and a very good distance swimmer, a former Olympic swimmer from South Africa named Graham Johnson, now living in Houston, who was far faster than anyone else in the long races. The rest of us were fighting for a bunch of second places.

If I had swum well I had a shot at second place—again—in every race. I didn't quite measure up. I did add a couple to my growing collection of second-place medals (the 50 and 100), and picked up two thirds (500, 1650) and a sixth (200). My sprinting was reasonably sharp, my distance racing dismal. Since I thought of myself as a distance racer and most of my training had been aimed at that end of the spectrum, I was a little disappointed.

I seemed to have missed my taper—I had been much more effective (and twenty seconds faster) for the East Coast Championships, three weeks before. But more than that, I had simply raced too much through the spring, overdoing it with competition as I had overdone it with training the previous fall. (The computer program didn't assess that factor.) I swam five 1650s in less than four months, improving through the first three, then deteriorating. By the time I came to the 1650 in the nationals—the last event of the four-day meet—I simply wanted to get the race over with and go home. I was getting a hard lesson in the numbing miseries of mental fatigue.

My heat of the 1650 was over a little after noon, and by four p.m. I was on the plane for home, as tired as I've ever been in my life. My talents as a nap-taker deserted me, and I sat staring out the window, trying to assess the meet, the year. I had swum my second-best times ever in three of the events (the 50, 100, and 500), but I had not improved a single time over the short-course nationals of the year before in Houston. My times averaged more than 1 percent slower than the year before, which was too much to blame just on aging, particularly with the volume of training I'd put in. I screwed up somewhere. To work my tail off for a year and not even hold my ground was too depressing to think about.

But my sprinting had held up just fine. I'd really nailed the 100 in particular, concentrating well, getting the mechanics right, attending to the details. I actually made up a little ground on Hill in the closing stages of the race. That was surprising. I really hadn't done much sprint training through the year. Maybe I should change my strategy a bit.

Maybe, I thought, I've about run out the string as a distance swimmer. Squeezing the few remaining percentage points out of my particular physiological package was going to require more work than perhaps I wanted to invest. From a health standpoint I'd gotten about all the gain I could expect. Maybe it was time to switch tracks, and see what I could accomplish as a sprinter.

The idea began to grow on me. I'd spent three years investigating the aerobic side of the equation, so to speak, learning about the problems of stamina and endurance. Why not take a look at the other side? Why not find out what there was to be learned about power and speed, about what's involved in trying to be quick? Here was this whole other aspect of athletics that I'd virtually ignored. Maybe there was some fun to be had there.

Then I remembered my stock response when friends asked why I didn't swim breaststroke, backstroke, or butterfly. I would start swimming the other strokes, I always said, when my freestyle stopped improving. Now, a full year without a single new personal best seemed to say I'd reached that point. The other strokes are never swum at distances longer than 200 meters; sprint training would pay off in those strokes too. Out of inexperience I'd be starting slow, and improving my times regularly as I picked up the skills. That would give me a psychological boost.

Besides, I'd have to learn them. I really wasn't much good at any of the strokes; each is a separate skill, an intricate and complex piece of coordination and timing. In a way that hadn't been required for freestyle, I'd have to find out a lot about motor learning. That was another subject that had always intrigued me, but that I'd never worked at very hard. How could I hope to understand athletics if I didn't investigate motor learning? And who knows, maybe I'd be good at the new strokes.

When the plane landed in Boston, I resented the interruption. It made me stop making notes for my new training plan. As I got off the plane I noticed I wasn't so tired anymore.

I never thought of it that way before, but I suppose this means that I am some kind of seeker—seeking a little more intensity, even from a bowl of ice cream. I earn my living in a "creative" business, which means only that I depend on ideas to pay the bills. So I seek ideas. They are usually small ones, God knows, but I pursue them professionally, the same way a baseball player pursues ground balls, the way my hand darts about beneath the surface of the pool seeking the purchase by which to pull myself forward. The moment when I find that purchase—the moment when an idea comes clear—is familiar to me; it comes with a *click*, followed by an involuntary grin. It is a moment of creative breakthrough, never mind the size or the quality of the creation. I think it is the same as the moment of athletic breakthrough.

I think the breakthrough comes in the fleeting moment when we have access to both kinds of consciousness, both kinds of thought, when the either–or, right–left nature of our usual mental state breaks open for a moment, and what was accessible only in one state becomes available to the other one. I think that peak performance has the same mechanism, the same physiology—metaphorical or otherwise—in any endeavor. I'll bet they eventually find the brain chemistry for it.

Those moments bring a warm rush of pleasure, even if it's only the miniature kick of a small new idea now and then. (Imagine the surge of joy from a really big idea. No wonder Archimedes dashed naked through the streets.) I am certain that it is the same satisfying jolt of pleasure from a well-hit shot in golf or tennis, from any successfully executed athletic movement—or from a vocal high note precisely rendered, a dance step that falls exactly on the beat. When it happens you are given full possession of a moment. (*That's* when time stops. Aging stops.) You are given a momentary glimpse of what might be possible, of what the human animal might yet fully be. You see new potential, which is the best antidote to aging there is. It is very addictive.

The mental state that precedes that burst of pleasure may be more addictive yet. It is the state of burning concentration that cuts through the noise of the world, that allows you finally to focus on the single thing—if you can only stay with it. That's what I am trying to learn. I am definitely addicted, the monkey on my back. Doing these things—training, racing, being an athlete—is the most productive way of pursuing that small, consistent joy that I've ever found. Doing these things has been the most fun I've ever had. Thinking about these things has made me happier than anything I've ever done.

# ACKNOWLEDGMENTS

Kenneth H. Cooper, M.D.; David L. Costill, Ph.D.; James E. Counsilman, Ph.D.; Jack Daniels, Ph.D.; E. C. Frederick, Ph.D.; Thomas A. McMahon, Ph.D.; and Michael Pollock, Ph.D.—distinguished scientists, every one of them—were extremely helpful to me in this project, and I am grateful to them.

I owe another very different gratitude to the people I have been competing with, and for, in the Valley Swim Club and the New England Masters Swim Club. I'm particularly grateful to a mixed group of individual swimmers, most of whom beat me regularly, all of whom helped and encouraged me, and inspired me by their own efforts: Barr Clayson, Fred Dalby, Mike Konstan, Jim Edwards, Darcy Fazio, Dick Guido, Ernie Hulme, Jim Johnsen, Dave McIlhenny, John Merril, Suzanne Rague, Bob Thomas, Stephanie Walsh, Win Wilson, Russ Yarworth, Bill Yorzyk, and my prime goad and maximum ergogenic stimulant, Tom Lyndon.

And then there was Bill Tyler, who turned me into a racer. I owe him most of all.